SEA OF FLAMES

Alistair Forrest

SEA OF FLAMES

Published by Sapere Books.

24 Trafalgar Road, Ilkley, LS29 8HH

saperebooks.com

ISBN: 978-0-85495-355-4

For my wife Lynda and our children Sebastian, Simone, Cassie, Corrine and Max.

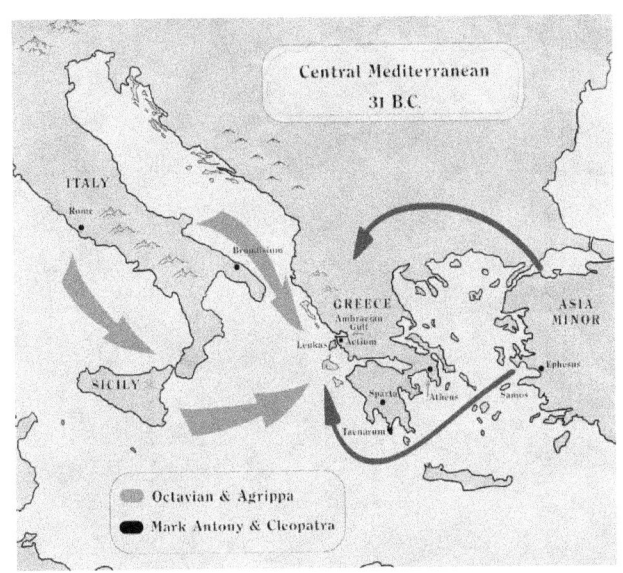

Central Mediterranean
31 B.C.

ITALY

Rome

Brundisium

GREECE
Ambracian
Gulf
Leukas Actium

SICILY

Spartal Athens

Taenarum

ASIA
MINOR

Ephesus

Samos

Octavian & Agrippa
Mark Antony & Cleopatra

PROLOGUE

Ephesus, Asia Minor, Winter 33BC

Lachares the Spartan knew something was wrong when Mark Antony wouldn't see him. Lachares had come all this way to Ephesus with military gear and weapons in four ships, braving winter storms. You would expect the great man to roll out a fancy carpet and open up his coffers, or the Egyptian queen's of course, not to mention his renowned stash of fine wines. Or even something stronger.

But no. He was left standing on the quayside like a Greek dummy in a world ruled by Romans — and Egyptians, apparently — with a motley array of client kings to help them rule the world. And to get into the harbour the four ships had dodged hundreds of impressive yet cumbersome Egyptian warships and transporters at anchor, sturdy giants of the sea attended by a swarm of impudent supply boats.

Did the queen have something to do with all this? Her money, everyone knew, was paying for this folly. And everyone also knew that Mark Antony wanted to show that whelp Octavian — son of a god, no less — just who should be First Man in Rome. Lachares had brought four boatloads of the finest weaponry to help him do it.

So what was the problem?

Lachares paced the dockside and looked longingly past a row of mean-looking harbour guards to the taverns on the far side of a busy street. Then he turned back to his crew. Faithful and hard-working, all of them. They had struck lucky, finding the wreck of a huge Egyptian vessel, survivors long gone to seek sensible refuge, and a valuable cargo that surely a general of Antony's standing would pay handsomely for. They had divided the cargo between their four smaller ships and made for Ephesus, where they knew good money was changing hands not just for supplies, but for weapons also.

So it was a shock when, instead of the Great Man himself, a rather nasty officer pushed through the ranks of guards, followed by four thuggish legionaries. His armour was ostentatious, a cuirass of fancy metalwork and a helmet adorned with plumage more befitting a peacock. He had a brutal square face like a block of granite. Cold, accusing eyes looked Lachares up and down, taking in the seaman's leather garb, unruly beard and wild matted hair, and the officer wrinkled his misshapen nose as if faced with vermin.

'You are Lachares the Spartan?'

'I am. Where's Mark Antony?'

The unpleasant officer gave him a look that indicated he need not impart such information. But Lachares knew that the struggle was no longer against Parthians and Armenians. Instead of the East, war now loomed against the West — with Octavian himself, who had stirred up the senate against Antony and his Egyptian queen, Cleopatra. The pair had proclaimed her teenage son Caesarion the true heir of the great Julius Caesar. And with all those losses in Parthia, Antony needed men — and weapons, which Lachares had brought in abundance.

The officer looked beyond Lachares to the four ships moored side by side.

'Stand aside.'

Lachares didn't move.

The officer turned his head and spat on the quayside, the men behind him reaching to their hips to grasp at swords.

Lachares stepped aside.

The officer walked towards the gangplank. Lachares found himself hoping the bastard would slip and fall into the murky harbour waters, where he would be crushed between the ship's flank and the quay's solid stone if he didn't drown first. But he proved to be nimble enough, and the ship's crew parted to allow the peacock aboard.

Let him inspect the cargo. He will soon see its value.

From where he waited ashore, Lachares could hear muffled orders below decks and the screech of rusty nails torn from damp wood as crates were opened. Then the officer reappeared briefly before leaping across to the next ship. Time passed, and Lachares felt sweat running down his back. He looked across to the taverns with the longing of a thirsty man after weeks at sea.

He heard his name being called and turned to see one of his captains, Myron, making his way across the bulwarks towards him. Despite his youth, he was the best of the captains and Lachares' right-hand man. He had a worried look on his face as he vaulted onto the quay.

'We've got trouble,' said Myron.

Lachares sensed this was not going to be his day. 'Go on.'

Myron pointed back towards the furthest of the four moored ships. 'That Roman thug has found the golden axe we hid in your cabin. He's asking awkward questions.'

Lachares cursed. He had hidden the axe to take home to Sparta as a trophy. The gold alone was worth a fortune, but the strange markings set it apart as some kind of ceremonial symbol of power. It probably belonged to a long-dead pharaoh. But he hadn't hidden it well enough, and now that Roman bastard was going to ask where he had acquired it —

not something he wanted to discuss with half the Egyptian court right here in Ephesus.

'Tell him it's not for sale. Make something up. Say it's a family heirloom handed down over the years.'

But the officer was already making his away across the decks, carrying what could only be the suspicious axe wrapped in cloths.

'Get back on your ship,' Lachares whispered to Myron. 'Have all four stand off until we know what's going on here. Put Ratboy ashore to watch from the shadows and if anything bad happens to me, get back home as fast as you can and tell my son what's going on.'

For a moment, Myron hesitated. He was not the type to leave a friend alone and in danger. But he saw the look in Lachares' eyes and jumped onto the nearest ship just as the Roman officer returned to the quay. From the corner of his eye, Lachares could see Myron talking to the child Ratboy, so named not just because his crooked teeth gave him the look of a rodent, but because his habit was to scurry about in dark places and learn the secrets of every crew member. The perfect spy is unseen and insignificant.

Ratboy leapt ashore and sauntered to a safe distance to watch as the officer squared up to Lachares. An oversized hand criss-crossed with scars moved the cloth aside to reveal a glittering axe head decorated with imprints of lordly figures and strange animals.

'Wasn't made in Greece, was it?'

'It belongs to my family and isn't for sale.'

The Roman's face was impassive. 'You wanted to meet with Mark Antony?'

Lachares said nothing.

'Then come with me.' To his men he barked, 'Close arrest!'

They marched him past the taverns with their tempting aromas of roasted meat and fresh bread and, more importantly, the spicy scent of Ephesian ale. Lachares' mouth was dry, his empty stomach groaning for food. He was marched past the forum and city baths to a huge courtyard before a lavish building, where a throng of gaily clothed citizens chatted merrily. Some leaned on huge pillars, while others mingled and laughed in the prelude to a war that everyone believed was Antony's for the taking. A band of musicians played the harp, pipes and drums, accompanying a choir of adolescents.

Most of these merrymakers fell silent when the scruffy sailor was marched in by a small squad of soldiers and chained to a post near the steps of the halls where the great and the good indulged in a feast, even though the sun was only just past its zenith. Those chains told Lachares he would have to think quickly and talk fast if he was to live another day. The officer left his men to guard the prisoner and stomped away towards the steps — presumably to see Mark Antony and his heretic queen.

One by one, the clusters of nobles and guests resumed their garrulous afternoon's leisure. The musicians found a louder tune to blot out the intrusion of a solitary prisoner, or perhaps to build the tension for entertainment to come. No one approached the unfortunate Lachares, who slumped beside the post and hoped that some merchant, or perhaps Antony himself, would soon appear to undo this travesty and restore him to his rightful place as a simple trader with a cargo to sell.

Ratboy slipped around the edge of the courtyard, watching. He took his chance and darted through a knot of laughing nobles and their garishly dressed women and slid on his knees next to the unfortunate Lachares.

'Your orders, Sir? Shall I free you?'

'Just wait. Hide yourself and watch. If they free me, recall the ships, but if they don't, report what you see to Myron.'

Ratboy nodded and scurried away. Lachares liked the boy and trusted him with his life.

He was watching where he went when the music stuttered and ceased, as did the hubbub and chatter. He lifted his gaze to the hall's entrance, where Mark Antony had made an appearance with Queen Cleopatra and her entourage. The queen was dressed simply; although her expensive dress shimmered with blues and silver in the sunlight, she wore no crown or diadem, and carried no mace of Egyptian royalty. Her right hand was draped casually on Antony's shoulder, and Antony was clearly drunk. While Cleopatra looked striking, he resembled a clown. He appeared to be dressed as Bacchus and held a goblet in his right hand. His gold earrings flashed, and his purple-fringed toga was streaked with wine-stains. Behind the Egyptian queen were the lovely handmaidens about whom paeans should be written. They were dressed in white and wore sufficient face paint to mask their expressions. Two of them Lachares knew to be Charmion and Iras, but the third? Surely she was the most beautiful. But what did beauty matter when he was on his knees before the two most powerful rulers of Rome's Eastern realms? Were these his saviours or his nemeses?

'We have entertainment for you all,' proclaimed Antony. 'Help me judge this man.'

He was slurring his words, and some of the nobles suppressed laughter. Everyone edged further away from Lachares, who saw that the brutish officer stood behind the self-made rulers of Greece, Asia and Egypt.

Antony reached behind him without looking, and the officer placed the ceremonial axe into his left hand. It wasn't heavy and had not been made for warfare, but it caught the sunlight and flashed wealth and history.

'This is the sacred golden axe of Seti!' he shouted. 'It was part of a consignment destined for your queen, Cleopatra Philopator, Bearer of the White and Red Crowns, mother of the heir to Caesar, joint ruler of the Eastern territories and your High Priestess! Yet it has fallen into the hands of a *pirate*. And that lowlife now cowers before us.' He pointed to Lachares. 'He has stolen her birth right and now seeks to profit from his crimes.'

The gasps all around him told Lachares his worst fears were about to be realised. He looked around for Ratboy and saw him crouching at the skirts of a large woman who was more interested in bloodshed than the proximity of a dirty child.

'Go,' he mouthed. 'Go now.'

But Ratboy was riveted to the spot, probably in denial.

'This man has offended my queen and offended the gods.' Antony was pointing at Lachares. 'He stole the sacred axe and he stole an entire consignment of valuables intended for our use. He is a pirate.'

The gasps now turned into shouts of judgement, demanding justice for such a crime. Everyone knew there was only one punishment, and everyone knew it would be better entertainment than tame music and idle chatter. They began to chant.

'Death, death, death!'

Lachares the Greek. No citizenship to fall back upon. A crowd baying for his blood, no chance to mount a defence. Again Lachares looked towards Ratboy, his eyes imploring him to leave. He didn't want him to witness the miscarriage of justice and bloodshed that was about to overwhelm his captain.

Lachares thought he saw a tear in Ratboy's eye. He tried to stand to protest, but Antony waved his right hand, forgetting it held a goblet. Crimson wine spilled as he gave his signal to proceed.

Two of the ruffians stepped forward, grasped Lachares' manacled hands, and twisted his arms backwards, which exposed the Greek's neck. The thuggish officer's hobnail boots made a 'clack, clack' sound on the stonework as he marched towards the bowed prisoner. He drew a *spatha* sword, holding it high. He looked around and saw bloodlust in the nobility of Ephesus. They counted.

'One, two, three.'

Everyone cheered as the long-haired merchant's head tumbled to the ground, spurts of blood discolouring the nearest togas and tunics, then pooling on the flagstones. They laughed. Everyone except Ratboy.

Antony raised his goblet and drank deeply. Cleopatra smirked. The handmaidens showed no emotion.

The crowd returned to their gossiping.

An execution was better entertainment than that wailing music.

PART ONE: THE QUEST

CHAPTER ONE

Taenarum, Peloponnesus. 32BC

Sometimes Ratboy was pure entertainment. But right now he was just plain annoying.

'That Mark Antony, doesn't he want our purple cloth? Thinks he's a king, he does. I could hide a dagger, get right up close and stab him in the heart.'

Eurycles chuckled. Apart from Ratboy, he was alone in his day office overlooking the bustling port, where he could work on the formal accounts while keeping watch on the approaches.

'You couldn't reach his heart. Stab him in the balls, more like.'

'Well, it's a start.'

'Then where would you be? They'd have your head off your shoulders quicker than you could say "Cleopatra's a witch".'

Ratboy went back to his brooding. Revenge was all the lad had talked about since returning from Ephesus. *To be fair*, thought Eurycles, *it's all I have thought about too, but you just can't walk up to a man like that and stab him in the heart. May the gods give me one opportunity. Just one.*

He missed his father. Myron had brought the ships back home to Laconia without their commander, and now Eurycles was an orphan. He didn't even have a mother to do all the weeping and wailing. But he was in his early twenties, a man, and if he had done one thing properly, it was learning how to trade Greek marble and purple dye. Maybe two things — he knew how to sail the small Laconian fleet, and he had the respect of the rower-warriors. Lachares had taught him well.

Eurycles put down his stylus. Enough calculations and accounts for one day. He gazed across the bay to the southernmost tip of Peloponnesus. There had been an abundance of shipping of late as there always was when war loomed, ships from Egypt and Crete in the south, Roman scout ships, Thracian traders — they all passed before Laconian eyes, and many sought shelter in his harbour. Some even sought wisdom from the Oracle of the Dead.

'Ratboy?'

'Yes, Commander?'

Eurycles laughed. 'No need for airs and graces here, when no one is around.'

'Sure, Commander.'

'Ratboy, do you know whose side we are on in the coming war?'

Ratboy shrugged. It was beyond him.

'Which of these Romans lays claim to Greece, Sparta and Laconia?'

The boy shrugged again.

'It's Mark Antony,' said Eurycles. 'He's going to want us to fight for him against Rome.'

'I ain't fighting for him. I told you, I will kill him.'

'Only if I don't get there first.'

Ratboy grinned. He dug into a pocket of his threadbare trousers and pulled out a coin, looked at it carefully, then passed it to Eurycles. 'Who's that?' he asked.

It was a silver denarius. Eurycles was quietly impressed that Ratboy had pilfered coin of his own. The boy was half his age and half his size yet had twice the nous. Eurycles turned the coin over in his hand. "Caesar Divi F" was stamped around the image of a man with wavy hair and a sharp nose.

'That's the new Caesar in Rome,' said Eurycles, handing the coin back.

'I'll fight for him, then,' said Ratboy with a sincere look.

'So will I,' said Eurycles.

He had found it hard to control his emotions since the news from Ephesus. He kept in mind that Ratboy had been the only Greek witness of the murder of his father, and somehow the boy's stoic determination helped him to keep an even keel, even in the darkest days.

Eurycles was dragged from his thoughts by Ratboy's squeaky, adolescent exclamation.

'We've got visitors.'

The ship making for the harbour showed no colours, but its rowers were disciplined. The crew had furled sail as the ship rounded the cape coming from the west and approached directly into the offshore breeze, white water creaming at its bows, the shrill of timing pipes making strange music with the rhythmical grunting of powerful oarsmen.

The harbour came alive. Opportunistic locals were setting up stalls, lighting firepits, rolling barrels of ale from the brewery, and setting up displays of pointless trinkets, most of which made ugly reference to the nearby Caves of the Dead. Musicians were competing for the best busking locations and one skeletal man, looking like he had just emerged from the underworld, was practising contortions that would be lucky to attract any coin whatsoever. The town's painted women were pouting and prancing in readiness for as many sesterces as they could acquire for dubious services.

'Romans?' Ratboy liked to sound like an authority on matters of the sea. He stood on the quayside with Eurycles and a handful of casually dressed dockers — uniforms, military or otherwise, were deemed unnecessary in Taenarum. They were there to trade, not to fight.

'Maybe Romans,' said Eurycles, shading his eyes from strong sunlight. 'But not navy. Can't see any weapons. A scout, maybe.'

The ship slowed as it passed the natural breakwater that had served the harbour well since time immemorial, oarsmen maintaining perfect rhythm even when slowing. They pushed forward as one to bring the vessel to a stop, with her bow just a spear's length from the quay. Eurycles hailed them.

'State your purpose here!'

A man of about thirty years came unsteadily to the command deck railings. His unruly hair blew in the breeze like wheat, framing a chubby, sunburnt face. He placed bulky forearms on the rail.

'Strabo. Geographer. Here to put your sweet haven on the map.'

A hooded man came to his side. Eurycles noticed how perfectly balanced he was as the ship rolled in a slight swell. Clearly a man used to the sea. None aboard seemed aggressive, so Eurycles called to the dockers to receive their mooring lines.

The hooded man came ashore first. Eurycles was always suspicious of men who concealed themselves in this way — the hood, to his mind, was a sign of secrecy — but he could see alert eyes and a wide, smiling mouth in the hood's shadow. And the man bowed deferentially, hands locked before him to show that no weapon would be drawn in anger. Priest? Diplomat? Servant? He didn't look like a servant. Behind him, Strabo was huffing and puffing with a bag of instruments.

'We seek Eurycles, son of Lachares,' said the hooded man.

'Who's asking?'

The hooded man looked around. He saw the activity around the harbour, which brought another smile, revealing strong white teeth with no gaps. *A good sign*, thought Eurycles. *Evil men always have teeth missing.*

'Someone who knows an injustice has been done. Where can we find him?'

'You'll have to tell me more. Then I will take you to him — if your purpose is peaceful.'

'We come in peace. I have a message for him.'

'So, your geographer is lying? It is not his mission, it is yours?'

'Oh, Strabo will be gone for hours if you let him roam. He's harmless.' As an afterthought, the hooded man added, 'As am I.'

I doubt that, thought Eurycles. 'Who sends Eurycles a message?'

'Caesar.'

'Caesar is dead. He has been these past dozen years or so. This is Greece; we don't care what you call your generals. But if they come back from the dead, yes, we're interested.'

'Have it your way,' replied the hooded man. 'The message is from Octavian.'

Eurycles realised this could be important, but he remained suspicious. 'Then we welcome you. But your men must leave all weapons behind. You will answer for your crew if they cause any trouble. There are taverns and inns aplenty in the town, but you will incur the wrath of Eurycles if anyone is harmed or if your men try to cheat our gentle community.'

'I vouch for the crew of my ship.' The man looked at the nearest inns and busy traders' stalls and took a few steps towards them, Strabo following. As he passed Eurycles, he leaned forward and said quietly, 'You can trust me, Eurycles. You may even become rich.'

Eurycles smiled. He liked the company of clever men.

Eurycles led both men to a backstreet tavern where a trusted landlord gave them a discreet table in the shade of an ancient olive tree and promised them the finest dishes and the best wine. He knew he would be rewarded as he always was when the son of Lachares came calling.

A shapely serving girl poured wine, her dress showing a hand's breadth of pale flesh at about nose height — always a test of the nature of men. Eurycles was pleased to note the hooded man paid no attention to this temptation, and neither did Strabo.

'Tell me,' said Eurycles, 'who brings this message from Rome?'

The visitor pulled back his hood, ignoring the cup before him, while Strabo drank deeply.

'My name is not important, but if we are to be friends, you can call me Marcus.' He, too, was about thirty, with the first signs of age showing beneath his eyes. He had a firm jaw with several days of dark stubble. Few had the opportunity to shave at sea in a cramped *liburnian*.

'Greetings, Marcus.' Eurycles was beginning to feel at ease. 'You are both welcome on our shores.'

The girl brought dishes of olives, cheese and bread, to which Strabo paid immediate attention, ignoring the pleasantries passing between Eurycles and his guest. Marcus was obviously the important one here; Strabo was more interested in his stomach than diplomacy. They chatted about the crossing from Brundisium — 'fair winds, calm seas. The gods were eager for us to find you' — and snippets of news from Italia, chiefly the senate's unease about the alliance between Mark Antony and the Egyptian queen. There were rumours that it would lead to war with Egypt, and there was an increase in warships and legions at Brundisium, Italia's closest port to Mark Antony's eastern territories.

Then, as a dish of grilled fish was served and wine cups were replenished, Marcus asked, 'Are you a pirate, Eurycles?'

There was a stony silence. Eurycles looked into Marcus's eyes and wondered if there was a more sinister purpose to this mission. Even Strabo stopped eating and looked from one to the other, his open mouth revealing a mush of white fish, some of which had found a home in his wispy beard.

'Why do you ask this?'

Marcus removed an olive stone and examined it thoughtfully. 'We have heard about your father.'

'My father was no pirate, just a merchant trader, as I am.'

'A smuggler, then?'

Eurycles grinned. 'Is there a difference? We avoid taxes where we can and seek the highest prices.'

'So what do you smuggle? Artefacts? Weapons? Slaves?'

'Never slaves. Goods only. Although sometimes rich people might pay us for passage. We never ask why.'

Strabo resumed his feasting, his attention turning to a dish of figs. Marcus sipped wine, then said, 'Octavian is of the opinion that your father's execution was a crime inspired by the Egyptian woman. We know Antony seeks war with Rome, but we also know he is in thrall to Cleopatra. What they did to your father was just one example of extremely un-Roman behaviour. Just one of many crimes. For months they have gathered Egyptian ships and Antony's legions to threaten Rome and before long they will be coming across the sea, all the way to Italia, and you Laconians will be right in the middle of the bloodiest war since the Persians came to Greece.'

Eurycles shrugged. 'What has this to do with a simple trader like me?'

Strabo, who had said nothing throughout this conversation, went to relieve himself. Marcus leaned closer, placing a hand on Eurycles' shoulder.

'You admitted you are a smuggler and that sometimes you provide passage for people who can afford it. Octavian can afford it.'

'Octavian wants to be smuggled out of Rome?' Eurycles regretted his words the moment they left his lips.

'Come, Eurycles, you are cleverer than that.'

'What then?'

'Antony and Cleopatra are gathered at Samos — you will know of this island. It's not far from Ephesus, where your father was murdered. There are some with him who have had enough and want to get out as fast as they can.'

'Defectors? Who?'

'First I need your solemn oath that you will be loyal to Rome in this matter, an oath that is easy for you to make because it is an opportunity to avenge your father, at least in part.'

'Put that way, I accept. My ships and my men are yours and Rome's. But tell me, Marcus, who are you to make such a request on behalf of the most powerful man in Rome?'

Marcus smiled. He touched the *fibula* brooch at his shoulder for luck. Eurycles absently took in the double-headed viper design and again wondered whether he was in the company of a friend or snake.

'Probably the second most powerful man in Rome,' Marcus said without a hint of modesty. 'My name is Marcus Vipsanius Agrippa.'

CHAPTER TWO

Strabo was bored. He wanted to explore this southernmost tip of Greece. He announced with a pompous flick of his head that he would find out as much as he could about this wonderful land, and then he wanted to go to Egypt to see for himself if the infamous Cleopatra was indeed a heretic as everyone said, or a noble pharaoh and the mother of great Caesar's heir.

At this, Agrippa laughed and announced cuttingly, 'If she is Egypt's queen, she should mind her own business in Egypt and leave the rest of the world to us Romans.'

'That, my dear Marcus, is the nub,' said Strabo. 'I suspect she will have quite some impact on our world before this dreadful war business is concluded.'

He turned on his heel and went to find a guide to show him the Caves of the Dead and face the horrors of Hades for himself. As he stomped off, Agrippa called out to him that if he wanted to return to Italia, he should not stray far from the harbour.

Eurycles took Marcus to the *laconica*, the baths for which the region was renowned, although he was apologetic because he had heard that bath houses in the great Roman cities were far better.

'Thanks for giving us the idea,' joked Marcus as they entered, making up for it by paying the attendant's fee. He took great delight in pointing out the phallic luck charm carved into the stonework. 'Too large to be Greek,' he smiled.

They steamed, they talked, and they cooled under buckets of cold water splashed over them by giggling women who were more used to Taenarum's flabbier citizens, but the implication of those admirations was banished with the icy flow. The conversation was of Ephesus, the island of Samos and what might be expected from an Eastern invasion force.

'From what we are hearing,' said Agrippa, 'Antony is taking his time. We know he wants to depose Octavian, but he seems more intent on celebrating a victory before his campaign has even got off the ground. The Egyptian queen has the money and is the driving force because her son is to be the new Caesar, and Antony has many client kings backing up his claim to be First Man, but where are the lovebirds? They're having a party on an island that he already controls, while his Roman generals twitch with distrust and even rebellion.'

Eurycles was no tactician, but as a Spartan he knew that every successful campaign hinged on decisive action, not fanciful theory.

'Who are the defectors?' he asked tentatively as they dressed, accepting cups of refreshing pomegranate juice from a servant.

'I'll come to that. But first, how well do you know Samos?'

'My ship, *Hera*, is named after the goddess of the island. That is her true home; she finds her way there in all weathers. I have been there several times, and I have good relationships with influential people who love our purple cloth.'

'Good, so you can sail there in, what, four or five days?'

'More or less, yes.'

'How soon can you leave? How many ships?'

'Just one. *Hera*. There's no threat from a single ship. Just a regular, friendly visit. I don't even have to use the harbour as there is a secluded bay near the city where my father was always made welcome by Samos fishermen.'

Agrippa's sideways glance and raised eyebrow needed no words. So, a smuggler after all. He was silent for several heartbeats, as if weighing up the options. 'Are you known to the authorities there?' he asked eventually. 'Or, for that matter, to Antony or his officers?'

'No. I was only ever a humble crewman, building muscle by rowing and hauling sail. My father took care of all business ashore.'

'Then you could sail *Hera* right into Samos harbour, if you were on official business? After all, you hail from one of the territories under the control of Mark Antony.'

It was Eurycles' turn to raise an eyebrow. 'What sort of business?'

'Oh, nothing alarming,' said Agrippa. 'It may surprise you to know that the Senate and Antony are still in the habit of exchanging messages, and I have several scroll cylinders for him and his senior officers. After all, we're all supposed to be Romans with a republic to govern. It would surprise you how structured warfare has become these days.'

'So would some of these messages be for the defectors?'

'Of course. They will want to reply, so they will ask you to wait on your ship. Then, probably after dark, they will quietly come aboard, no fuss, and you can bring them back here, where I will arrange onward passage to Rome.'

It sounded very straightforward to Eurycles. He was young but not stupid. What was it his father had said? *Always expect the unexpected.* That hadn't saved his father, and now he was being asked to undertake a dangerous mission right under the nose of the crazed executioner himself. He was to pledge himself to Rome's cause, then thumb his nose at her deadliest enemy. You don't put your hand into a nest of vipers and expect to live.

'I'll do it,' he heard himself say.

Eurycles hadn't always been quite so eager to throw himself in the way of danger. In many respects his early life had been sheltered by protective parents, who unlike their friends had not been blessed by the gods with a household brimming with noisy children. Just the one, born amid the blood and screams of a horrendous birth. But there was Spartan blood in the child's veins.

A tutor who happened to be an ageing Olympian recognised a latent spirit of adventure in young Eurycles and taught him basic wrestling holds, before realising that speed of thought was matched by his speed in a sprint. On many occasions, this had got him out of trouble with Taenarum's bigger — and slower — youths. His mother, Selene, ravaged by illness since the boy's birth, did her utmost to keep him away from danger while his father Lachares was away at sea. Although he loved his mother dearly, Eurycles had a mind of his own and learned the hard way to avoid broken bones and the mental injury of insults and contemptuous mockery. He saw a quiet strength in his mother. The lines around her eyes and mouth and the greying at her temples failed to fully disguise what had once been a vision of loveliness that would turn the head of any man — a beauty of which she was completely unaware, despite the rapt attentions of her devoted husband.

Her sickness was all Eurycles' fault. He had overheard his parents explaining to the doctor that since the child's birth, the vivacious Selene had been weighed down by the demons of pain, grief and distress, beyond even the power of the gods — let alone the doctor. But Spartans didn't give in. She went to work in the town's biggest inn, first in the kitchens, then serving at tables, always with a smile and a kind word that belied her inner pain.

It was in that very inn that a teenage Eurycles made his first move into true manhood and set himself on a path that one day would catch the eye of the great Roman admiral, Marcus Vipsanius Agrippa. He was hauling sacks of vegetables to the inn's kitchens, carrying flagons of ale and wine for the genial host, and trying not to get under the feet of the cooks and serving girls. The inn was unusually busy that night, looking after the crews of two Thracian ships bound for Cyrenaica with a cargo of timber. The men wanted more than a pot of stew, ale and half-decent wine. It was noisy, raucous and chaotic. Taenarum had its fair share of painted women, but as the night wore on and the singing became more and more incoherent, there were some Thracians who became more than a little concerned their needs might not be met because the youngest and prettiest were already taken.

That was when a handful of middle-aged sailors became bored with their game of dice and noticed the attractive Selene as she served their table. The haze induced by too much wine faded the lines of worry and pain on her face. Her modest dress merely hinted at a slim figure and when a hand was placed where it shouldn't have been, she maintained her smile. That was a mistake.

Eurycles, who had been sent by the host to clear bowls from the tables, was directly behind his mother when this happened. Without hesitation, he took hold of the offending wrist, squeezed firmly at the base of the thumb, and wrenched the hand away. This produced a yowl of pain from the man, whose eyes were rimmed red and whose beard dripped with wine. He had been drinking from his cup while in the process of making his intentions known. The table fell silent. Selene turned to her son and ordered him out of the room. *Now. I can handle this*, her eyes said.

The man with red eyes stood clumsily and clouted Eurycles on the side of the head. Selene shouted, 'Stop!' but three other men also rose. They were about to speak their minds to this impudent youth, but they didn't get the chance. Eurycles punched the red-eyed man on his bulbous nose, and spurting blood signalled a free-for-all. Eurycles barely had time to tell his mother to get out before a punch glanced off the side of his shoulder. The man with red eyes had collapsed in a heap on the floor, out of it. That left three bulky sailors against one lithe but not particularly muscular fifteen-year-old. His tutor had taught him about how the human body lives and breathes and for a moment, before he went down under the weight of flailing fists and beefy torsos, Eurycles focused on the nearest man's throat and jabbed hard with straight fingers, then swivelled his elbow to crush sinew and bone on the bridge of the next man's nose.

Fifty heartbeats later he was left pummelled and bruised outside the inn, lying in a street of vomit, piss and discarded food scraps. There was a knife embedded in his thigh, the blood pooling black in the filth.

But one Thracian was dead and two others would not be well enough to crew their ship across the sea to Cyrenaica.

There was another casualty, though.

Selene, unable to come to terms with the violence that left her only son scarred and bedridden, was dead within a year. And Eurycles, still a teenager, had yet more guilt laid on his skinny shoulders.

CHAPTER THREE

Eurycles had never heard of Lucius Munatius Plancus or his nephew Marcus Titius. These were the names dropped by Agrippa like a pair of coins tossed into a beggar's bowl as if everyone would know who or what they were. As if their very names would make him want to risk his life to smuggle them away from Mark Antony.

So Eurycles shrugged.

Agrippa had spent the second day touring the harbour and the town's scant fortifications. He hadn't needed to explain to Eurycles why Taenarum was important to Rome as it was plain as day that Egyptian grain ships and reinforcements would pass this way the moment Mark Antony made his westward move. Cut off the gateway to the Ionian Sea and Antony would have to find alternative supply lines across inhospitable mountains.

As the heat of day eased, they boarded Agrippa's ship and now reclined in his remarkably comfortable quarters built forward of the steering platform. Eurycles admired the modifications to a classic *liburnian*, including a partial deck above the rowers' benches on which awnings had been erected as sleeping quarters for when the crew returned from their run ashore. Ratboy was running errands, first bringing a flagon of local wine then negotiating with a dockside street-seller for his finest spit-roasted mutton wrapped in flatbread.

Agrippa chewed appreciatively, ignoring the grease that dripped from his chin. 'All I've done since arriving here is eat and bathe,' he muttered through a mouthful, then got to the point. 'Plancus is old, fat and infirm, but he has plenty of money and knows full well that if Antony and Cleopatra lose this war, he risks losing his estates in Italia.' He swallowed, holding up a finger. 'And he has a history of changing sides on a whim.'

'Then why would you trust him?' asked Eurycles.

'Trust Plancus? Never. But he may have something of value. You see, when he wrote to us in the last despatches from Ephesus, he dropped a hint that he had helped Mark Antony write his will, and Octavian would love to know more about that!'

Eurycles gave him a puzzled look. 'Are wills not sacrosanct in Rome?'

'That depends on who's looking.' Agrippa smiled and left it to Eurycles to fill in the gaps. He then described the nephew Titius as an arrogant, driven cavalry officer who considered himself a gift from the gods to the people of Rome. He was a ladies' man who lived dangerously and whose enemies invariably met violent death at the hands of cutthroats in dark alleys.

Initially, Eurycles had felt the thrill of the challenge, but now he was wondering how he might pull off such a daring mission. It was fairly simple if the defectors were anonymous lesser mortals, but Plancus and Titius were apparently a scheming politician and his murderous nephew. Not the sort of company he would choose for the long voyage home on *Hera* after a dangerous extraction under the nose of his father's executioner. It was not too late to pull out, refuse Agrippa and live the quiet life of a cloth merchant.

Eurycles took a deep breath and heard himself promise Agrippa that he would do this, heard Agrippa's reply that he wouldn't regret his decision and made a mental note that Rome's foremost general would return to Taenarum on the *kalends* of Quintilis to relieve Eurycles of his infamous passengers. He had twenty days to sail into the lion's den and bring back two dubious characters, all the while trying not to ruin the mission by attempting to exact revenge on Mark Antony. At least, not yet.

But he couldn't do it alone. He would need the help of a good crew and his most trustworthy captain.

He sent for Myron.

Ratboy found Myron watching a golden sunset from the terrace of his mother's house at the back end of town. He appeared to be lost in thought and didn't move as the boy approached from behind. But no one caught Myron unawares.

'This had better be important, Ratboy,' he said without turning.

'How did you know it was me?'

Myron kept his gaze on the sunset. 'Because for a little chap you make enough noise to raise the dead. Besides, I can smell you a mile away.'

Ratboy was used to the insults. He would have been offended if Myron or any of the crew treated him differently. Sailing the Middle Sea with these men was his life — they were his only family.

'The commander wants to see you.'

Still watching the sunset, Myron asked, 'Does he now? What about?'

'I think he wants you to go and kill Mark Antony.'

Myron turned to face Ratboy. Barely older than Eurycles, his face was bronzed and etched by the sun, as with all sailors of the Middle Sea. There was not one *uncia* of fat on his lithe, thin body. He was a man Ratboy and all Taenarum crew would follow anywhere, against monsters of the sea or the legions of Rome.

He laughed. 'Go and find my mother and ask for a cup of citrus water. Then let's go and find out what Eurycles really wants.'

Refreshed, Ratboy led Myron through dusty streets, pushing aside indignant locals and dodging the last of the day's fruit-sellers, who were waving away flies. They hurried past the shambolic agora, which fronted the equally undisciplined local *prytaneum*, where pigeons nested in capitals and friezes. By day it was a setting for harbour business and impromptu stalls of local wares, the place to gather for news and gossip; now it was sparsely populated by the evening's scavenging birds.

Agrippa seemed pleased to see Ratboy back again; everyone loved his infectious pluckiness and undeniable cheek. Myron followed him into the cabin. A nod and a grunted greeting were all that was expected of seasoned sailors.

'We sail tomorrow,' announced Eurycles who knew Myron was not one for wasting time on formalities. 'Our mission is to extract two defectors from Samos, where Mark Antony has gathered his forces.'

'Understood.' Myron was not the type to question orders.

'One ship. *Hera.* When can you provision?'

Myron swiftly calculated crew readiness and the weapons they would need, as well as food and water. They could make short hops to Melos, Naxos and Icaria for rest and more provisions, and reach Samos in four days with a westerly — six without.

'We can be ready by the fourth hour.'

'See to it.'

Myron turned to leave.

'Wait,' said Agrippa. Myron turned back. 'Don't you have any questions? Don't you want to know what this is all about?'

Myron did not mince his words. 'Sir, I know who you are, and I know that Mark Antony will bring his forces to Peloponnesus and Greece. There are many city states here, but this one is opposed to Antony. Our ships and our swords are yours, as I am sure Eurycles has told you.'

Agrippa was impressed. 'He has indeed. Is this the view of your men also?'

'Sir, we loved Lachares and mourn his loss still. We fight for Rome.'

'Thank you, Myron,' Eurycles interjected. 'Dismissed.'

When the Greek captain had left, Eurycles shooed out Ratboy, who had taken all this in and turned to Agrippa. 'What else do we need to know?'

'It's more what I need to know,' said Agrippa. 'I have a network of informers across our territories, but sadly too few in Ephesus, Samos and Asia. My people — spies, if you like — keep me informed throughout Gaul, Spain, Africa and Greece. They wear a badge of honour.'

He touched the double-headed viper brooch at his shoulder.

'I will give you one of these and another should you find someone worthy. All who wear this *fibula* pledge their loyalty to me, and thence to Rome. It is dangerous work, and only for those who put Rome's interests above their own lives. Will you wear this?'

'Gladly,' said Eurycles. 'For my father.'

'Good man. We will meet again on the *kalends*, and if I know anything about you, your captain Myron and this Ratboy creature, I think I may have more *viperae* to appoint!'

'We are honoured. We won't disappoint. We have business with Antony.'

Agrippa yawned. 'Two more things, before we drink to your success. Take Strabo with you. He may be a bit of a bore at times, but he knows the region you're going to, and he has family in Asia.'

'As long as he's not a liability.'

'Well, he's no sailor, and he's certainly no soldier. But Antony has alliances with the kings of that region and Strabo has a good understanding of how they think. It may come to nothing, but it's as well to have his experience on this mission.'

Eurycles nodded his agreement. 'You said, two things?'

'I did. Again, it may come to nothing, but watch out for Lucius Gellius Publicola. If you meet him, run the other way. Or kill him.'

Eurycles raised an eyebrow. He was enjoying Agrippa's company, despite his dire warnings.

'I expect you are going to tell me why.'

CHAPTER FOUR

The gods were kind. Zephyrus blew briskly from the west, filling *Hera*'s sails, while Poseidon withheld the swell that causes ships to slew and plunge. She was the envy of the region's pirates, none of which could catch her, especially in flat seas like this with the strange, outrigged sails that Myron was using to harness the following wind. From ahead or astern, she must have looked like a giant seabird skimming the water. All of the ports and islands in this part of the Aegean Sea knew *Hera* for her distinctive purple sails and turn of speed, whether under sail or oars. And right now, her rowers relaxed, played dice, chatted, slept. They were not needed.

Eurycles was content to leave the ship under Myron's command, and since leaving Icaria, where they had beached for the third night of their journey, he had found his preferred place in the bows to watch a pod of dolphins showing the way to nearby Samos. He always found this hypnotic. His ship and the sleek fish surged together, the creatures oblivious to the worry that men felt when war loomed. For the hundredth time he contemplated the strange mission, and for the hundredth time he could not come near to imagining what awaited him.

Behind them on the steering platform, Myron concentrated hard despite the attentions of Ratboy beside him. Above them, the blue-and-gold figure of the goddess watched over their course to Samos, which now lay ahead like a low cloud on the horizon. Nothing could distract a captain who left little to chance, not flotsam in the water ahead nor an injudicious turn that could see the widespread sails catch a wave and drag the ship into trouble. He ignored the men beside him, who were laughing and singing, encouraged by Ratboy. There was deep-voiced Niko with his infectious smile and Shoeless Luka, who preferred this day to wear no clothes whatsoever. On land they were perfectly normal citizens, at sea, joyous children. They tossed pieces of Icarian bread high to see if acrobatic gulls this far east could catch as well as their cousins back home. Each success was celebrated with a carefree jig.

Strabo joined Eurycles in the bows. Unlike Shoeless he wore a loose, full-length tunic, stained at the front with the remnants of last night's dinner. He clutched at the bow rail. The ocean was not his natural habitat.

'I envy them,' he said, pointing at the frolicking dolphins. 'No cares, not like us.'

Eurycles grunted. The nearer he got to Mark Antony, the more he felt the weight of his father's death crushing him.

'What cares do you have?' he asked Strabo.

'I left home when I was young because I wanted to see the world and write. Going west, I felt light and free. Coming back east, it feels heavy.'

'It feels dark for me too.'

Strabo put a hand on Eurycles' shoulder. 'Your first time here since, you know…'

Eurycles said nothing. The truth was, it hurt. At least he wouldn't have to go to Ephesus, where he would probably see his father's blood on the ground.

'Some people say the East is so much more civilised,' Strabo went on, 'but it's not. They will chop off your hand for stealing a loaf of bread. Stone a woman for looking at a man.'

'Oh, we have our injustices in Greece, and from what I hear in Rome too.' Eurycles turned to Strabo and smiled ruefully. 'Perhaps it will all change when this coming war is concluded?'

'Doubt it,' snorted Strabo.

But Eurycles was no longer listening. He was looking across towards Samos, now a much clearer outline on the horizon. There was movement. Slow, lazy movement in the haze. He turned, fingers to his mouth, gave a shrill whistle to attract Myron's attention, and pointed ahead. Myron was already peering through the gap between the mainsail and the gullwings.

'Antony?' Eurycles called.

'Who else?' Myron replied.

The crew, alerted, strained to look towards the distant island. The shapes could only be ships, but so many? Everyone knew war was coming, and now they were witnessing its onset; at least fifty large vessels were on their port quarter, probably making for Athens. Eurycles thought, *Are we too late?* But then he had heard that between them, Mark Antony and Cleopatra had upwards of three hundred ships, and this might be only the first wave. Still, they would have to hail the lead ship as they carried senate messages for several dignitaries, and the two officers they had been sent to collect may already have left Samos.

They closed at speed. Eurycles could soon see that these were large ships, slow leviathans, probably Egyptian. He effected a small change of course to point *Hera* to the lead ship and ordered the crew to their rowing stations once they had hauled in the side sails. The sailors worked deftly, stowing the furled sails and taking their positions with oars inboard but placed ready in their tholes. The ship slowed to a steadier speed under main and foresail only; the dolphins left to find better entertainment.

'Stand by pipes!'

Myron's order was for Ratboy. He was not merely the ship's boy for menial tasks, but also the one who piped the rhythm for the rowers. He was an accomplished piper and had learnt many a lively tune in the alehouses and inns of Taenarum and the rowers loved his unusual melodies and mischievous off-key notes, not to mention his comical expressions. Ratboy rummaged in his sack of belongings and returned to his position on the steering deck, clutching twin reed pipes favoured by Peloponnesian shepherds. A hundred rowers stared back at him, most pulling faces, some suggesting a favourite tune which invariably invoked ribald lyrics in the minds of sailors a long way from home.

Myron focused on the foremost vessel ahead. Eurycles, remaining in the bows, strained to see what colours these ships bore, though he did not know if Mark Antony or Cleopatra had any distinguishing pennants. His own streamed blue, Greece's colour. An ally. And there was no mistaking the large eye painted on *Hera*'s bows. Eurycles knew that Egyptian vessels often carried the Eye of Horus in the hope of seeing the way ahead. In all, no threat. And it was just one small ship approaching the many.

The gap closed. He ordered the mainsail furled and oars out. Ratboy began a gentle tune, just to keep way. No rush, no threat.

The lead ship was enormous. It had no Egyptian decoration; it was just a lumbering troop carrier looming ever higher, dwarfing *Hera*. There were three decks of oars so large that Eurycles thought they must have been manned by several rowers each. They moved in a slow and deliberate circular motion, the dull thud of a timing drum contrasting menacingly with Ratboy's shrill pipes. Her waterline streamed with green weed, her flanks bleached white by years in the summer sun. Although just a few hours out of Samos, she smelled like a barracks latrine.

Grim-looking officers on the steering platform paid *Hera* scant attention, so Eurycles gave a hand-signal to Myron to sail past. He pointed to the next ship in the haphazard formation, a smaller quinquereme, though still three times the size of *Hera*.

This time there was interest in their approach. Three uniformed officers, helmetless, came to the railings and watched the small Greek ship approach. Myron knew what to do to make an impression. He barked an order to increase speed while simultaneously giving deft hand-signals to his steersmen, Shoeless Luka and Niko. The watching officer on the quinquereme became agitated. At the last minute, just feet from the dipping oars, a command from Myron had the starboard oars plunged down steady and the paddle rudders hard over. One final pull by the port rowers and *Hera* slewed impossibly around, parallel to the quinquereme, facing in the same direction. In the spaces between decks, anxious faces peered across the short distance. These were men who knew the havoc that could be caused if the impudent ship had collided with their oars, each thrusting into chest or back on impact to cause devastating injuries. The quinquereme's crew had stopped rowing in their moment of fear, hoping this wasn't some ignorant pirate ending their careers or worse, their lives. Each now looked relieved.

The officers were angry. They said nothing, but just glared.

Eurycles danced across the rowing benches to the stern platform and stood next to Myron, a naked Shoeless, a smiling Niko and young Ratboy. They must have looked like pirates.

'*Hera* out of Taenarum bearing messages for Mark Antony and his officers.'

The officers looked as though they had trodden in dog's mess in the street.

'Messages from who?' one of them called.

'Some bear the Senate's seal, others … who knows? Wives and lovers who miss their Roman heroes?'

The same officer spat over the rail. He seemed uncertain whether Eurycles was being sarcastic, and when you are a tough officer and don't know how to react, you spit.

'Your ship is Greek, not Roman.'

Eurycles held his hands wide. 'Does it matter? We are paid to deliver, and that's what I'm doing.'

'Ship oars and throw a line,' said the officer. He pointed at Shoeless. 'And tell that clown to put some clothes on.' He turned to bark orders to his own crew.

It took some time to bring the smaller ship alongside, but the swell was light and *Hera* was in the lee of the quinquereme. Ratboy brought Shoeless a tunic which he reluctantly pulled on. When a rope ladder was dropped over the side of the quinquereme, it became evident that at least two of the officers were going to inspect *Hera*. Only to be expected. None of the crew was armed, but Eurycles did not sense there would be any trouble as long as the visitors didn't start it.

They didn't, but they came close. The first officer down was the one who had done all the talking. He was clutching a vine stick which marked him out as a centurion. It wasn't easy to negotiate the ladder in hobnail boots — the Laconian sailors had learned long ago that light canvas shoes with rope soles were essential at sea — and the *gladius* at his hip snagged several times, while the vine stick was a further encumbrance. He crunched onto *Hera*'s deck and scowled. A second officer with the same swarthy features followed. *Army ruffians*, thought Eurycles, *definitely not seamen*. He ought to salute, offer a steadying hand, and maybe call for refreshments. But not for these sour brutes.

'Show me.' The centurion's eyes flicked around the gathered crew, seeing only indifference, then alighted with cold intensity on Eurycles, who smiled disarmingly.

'You're standing on it.'

'Huh?'

'You're standing on the hold hatch.'

The centurion looked down and saw that he stood on a large hatch with a sunken iron ring built into the port side of the steering platform's deck. On the other side of the platform was its twin. He grunted and stepped aside. Niko made a big show of heaving it upright. The officer peered into the shadowy hold and saw a dozen bolts of cloth, neatly stacked. Beside them was a scattering of spears and swords. The officer looked at Eurycles as if he was being taken for a dim-witted fool.

'They don't look like messages to me. It looks more like you're looking for a fight. And what's with that fancy cloth?'

Eurycles thought about putting a friendly arm around him and promptly decided against it. 'We're merchants, not soldiers. The cloth is for sale to…' He thought about saying *to people far richer than you*, but wisely dismissed that folly. 'To the court of the Egyptian queen.'

'Good luck with that. So where are these messages?'

'In the other hold.'

Shoeless sniggered and the centurion fought to control his temper. 'Bring them to me. Now!'

The second hatch was opened and Shoeless leapt into the gloom. Soon, a strongbox was being hauled onto the deck.

'Open,' said the officer.

Shoeless worked the latch, began to open it, then slammed it shut in apparent alarm. 'Snakes and scorpions!' He grinned like a maniac when the Roman recoiled. Then he noticed the man's bunched fist and a raised vine stick and promptly threw the lid open. The centurion scowled and peered in.

What he saw was ten scroll cylinders. All bore an official seal. Four of them bore the name M. Antonius. Others bore the names Amyntas of Cappadocia, Tarcondimotus of Cilicia, Quintus Dellius, Gnaeus Domitius Ahenobarbus, Lucius Munatius Plancus and Marcus Titius. The truth was, Eurycles had no idea who half of these people were and would deliver them to an army quartermaster for distribution, except for the cylinders marked Plancus and Titius, of course. Mission accomplished, apart from secretly extracting the latter two defectors and delivering them to Agrippa.

He had guessed the names he was unfamiliar with were in fact also likely defectors who just needed the idea of a better life in New Rome sowed in their minds. So this brutish Roman officer was looking into a strongbox containing a number of messages that could change the course of the war, and if he dared break the seals and read the contents, *Hera*'s entire crew potentially faced mass execution. Given that Eurycles knew the contents of the messages to Plancus and his nephew, the enormity of the next few moments suddenly dawned him.

Then another fact dawned on him as he saw the way the centurion was looking at the names written large on each scroll.

This man can't read.

He decided to help him out.

'As you can see…' he began and sensed that momentary relief that no one can fully disguise when caught in an embarrassing moment. 'As you can see, these four are for Mark Antony himself, and these others are for his most trusted generals and allies. Probably just legal documents and news of their estates over in Italia.'

The centurion nodded slowly, hoping he wasn't being hoodwinked and beginning to wish he hadn't got involved.

'So,' continued Eurycles brightly, 'where can I find Mark Antony and all these *very important* generals? Are they on one of these ships? Have they gone ahead, or are they still on that island over there?'

The officer seemed puzzled. Here he was, trying to act like a vital cog in in a massive operation, but the look on his face indicated that he would rather be somewhere else. He grunted and waved his vine stick in the vague direction of Samos harbour.

Eurycles persisted. 'If they have left Samos, where are all these ships going?'

This was a much more relevant question to an army man used to the logistics of moving an invasion force across vast distances to defeat an enemy.

'Athens, of course,' said the centurion, now sensing a warmer relationship with the Greek merchant. 'We're to join the Macedonian legions.'

'And then?'

The centurion smiled for the first time, although with his thin lips and crooked teeth it seemed more of a pained grimace. 'What do you think? We put our man in his rightful place in Rome.' With that, he concluded the inspection, probably realising he had said too much, Greek ally or not. 'Be on your way, and good luck selling your cloth. Those Egyptians will fall over themselves for it, and they've plenty of gold.'

Ratboy, Shoeless and Niko put on a comical performance as the two men climbed their ladder, bowing dramatically and thumbing noses to raucous applause from the watching quinquereme crew. As the lines were released and *Hera* drifted apart, Shoeless lifted his tunic and presented sun-bronzed hindquarters as a final salute, eliciting a barrage of returned insults, jeers and hurled debris.

Laughing, Strabo slapped Eurycles on the back. 'If that's Antony's finest, Octavian has nothing to worry about. Let's go find our defectors.'

CHAPTER FIVE

The woman exuded calm assurance, confident in her effect on men, especially those in authority at Samos port. She was in her mid-twenties, and there was a look in her kohl-rimmed eyes that warned others not to disrespect her. She had a firm jaw, a wide, quirkily lopsided mouth, dark hair pinned with colourful beads, and a slim, boyish body. She wore a sheer dress that covered her frame from neck to ankle, and was made from dazzlingly smooth fabric. A silver-threaded shawl was tied at her waist. Though not an Egyptian, her authority came from the Queen of Egypt herself.

Her fine clothes contrasted with the pervading stench of rotting fish, profusely sweating slaves, and fly-infested dung dropped by a procession of pack animals and lumbering oxen that hauled outsized carts. This was nothing she wasn't used to, since she had spent her childhood in the Asian provinces. Though a woman in a man's world, she neither expected nor received any challenge to her power in the filthy trading port. She was overseeing the provisioning of an enormous galley moored stern-on to the dock, as close landward as an excessive draught would allow. The cacophony of shouted orders and curses, the groaning of vast pulleys used to load jostling transporter ships, and the cries of hungry gulls all assaulted the senses of this olive-skinned beauty as she checked the manifest for the Egyptian flagship *Antonia*.

The name she went by, Zara, was abbreviated from Zaramandukht — the name given to her by parents who curried favour with the region's kings. These all ruled in Mark Antony's provinces, and thus a long-limbed girl with a regal name swiftly came under the gaze of the Roman Triumvir's paramour, Cleopatra VII Philopator. Even disdainful Mark Antony had commented on her talents. 'A better man than any of my tribunes,' he had laughed. 'And far prettier.'

But Zara knew too much and wished she didn't. She tried to keep a low profile, but that wasn't easy for such a striking woman blessed with intelligence. Time and again she had stood up to officious Romans who had no respect for her, especially those who believed her place was in the bedroom, not waving authority in their faces. The worst was Mark Antony himself. She had been just a few weeks in Cleopatra's employ in Ephesus when she had witnessed the execution of a Greek sailor on trumped-up charges of piracy, and she had begun to wonder whether she was in the wrong place at the wrong time. Then there was a procession of suitors, all misogynists bearing the insignia of Roman greatness. Never mind their wives back home; they believed Zara should spread her legs on demand.

She had handled it well with Cleopatra's help. A mute bodyguard had deterred many until his mysterious murder sometime during the short voyage to Samos. An anchor or large rock strapped to a man's feet and dropped overboard was the common method of removing hindrances. And she knew who was behind it; she just couldn't prove it. And now that murderous bastard was striding towards her on the dockside.

Zara groaned inwardly as Marcus Titius approached. She knew what he was capable of. This man thought nothing of executing officers on a whim and had been the man who had shown the fleeing Sextus Pompey no mercy after his failure in the Sicilian wars. And of late he had seemingly decided that she would be a suitable mistress. His astonishing arrogance had even led him to boast that he could free her from the tyranny of a heretic queen and give her a life of wealth and power in

Rome. A boast that revealed his intention of switching sides as soon as the opportunity presented itself. She had kept that knowledge to herself, pretending she didn't understand what Mark Antony's officer was implying. She hoped that he had not found out that she, too, harboured doubts about the folly she saw all around her.

But he was pushy then and he was pushy now. It was worse when he had company because he liked to impress his men, and on this occasion he had a tall officer with him. Zara knew that he had already told the man that she was panting for his manhood.

'Lady, I am here to assist.' Titius flashed what he thought was his winning smile.

'How kind, but I don't need any help.'

Zara immediately turned to the servants who were loading a provisions pallet and busied herself checking the sacks on her lists. Her back was to Titius and he was outraged.

'I spoke to you, woman. Do not turn your back on me!'

She turned. She gave her best withering stare and knew that she had made an enemy. No man liked to be rebuffed, especially this one, whose eyes flashed venomously.

'Can you not see I'm busy?'

From the corner of her eye, she sensed a small incoming vessel was docking in the space left by a departing troopship. It registered because the traffic was until now all one-way, ships departing for Athens. She dismissed it as inconsequential, although she liked the way the sailors leapt deftly onto the quayside to moor their ship. Definitely Greek. Hopefully they were better company than this boorish young Roman, who clearly wanted to strike her but could not in the company of one of his officers. She stared at him defiantly. Titius stared back.

'Do you not realise that you need a man's help?' Titius leaned closer so that others nearby could not hear. 'Life is different in Rome, and you will need a good man to look after you.' Titius was not a tall man, but what he lacked in size he made up for with arrogance and bravado. Zara just stared at him angrily, her eyes level with his.

'I'll let you know when I find one.'

She knew it was folly to speak thus. She was not a Roman citizen and Titius was unpredictable. He would suffer no consequence if he beat her, whipped her or even killed her. But she trusted Anahit, whose bracelet she wore — dragon devouring dragon in a perfect circlet — and she trusted herself. She knew it was not her time to suffer or die. Not yet.

Titius grasped her wrist, crushing the bracelet against her bones, but she did not wince and held his angry gaze. Her companions and assistants shrank back. If this had been an Egyptian aggressor, they would have clubbed him to death, but not a Roman. They knew the consequences.

'You will do as I say,' he rasped.

'I will not. Let me go. I have work to do.'

Titius turned to his companion for support. The tall officer smiled, no doubt grateful that it was not he who was in this predicament. His smile lacked respect. Titius twisted his grip, but Zara didn't flinch. Then he sensed a crowd was forming. He looked around. There were three men and a child staring at him. One man wore a stained, ankle-length tunic. The other men were clearly sailors, unshaven and dishevelled, smelling of the sea and clearly all in need of the baths. Two of them carried a chest by its rope handles. The child was grinning, hopping from one foot to the other as if something exciting was about to happen. So Titius let go of Zara's wrist and turned to face them.

'Who are you?'

'Visitors from Taenarum,' said Eurycles. 'Bearing messages from the Senate in Rome.'

'Is that so? Hand them over, then.'

Eurycles studied the Roman and decided he wouldn't trust him, however high up the pecking order he might be. 'Perhaps you would be good enough to direct us to the offices of Mark Antony?'

Titius bridled and began to square up to Eurycles with an unpleasant scowl when Zara spoke.

'Strabo?'

She was looking at the scruffy geographer with wide eyes. It was a look of complete amazement. She said again, louder this time, 'Strabo? Is it really you?'

Strabo, who had hung back from the developing confrontation, bore a puzzled expression that slowly transformed into recognition.

'Zara?'

Strabo hadn't seen his younger sister in years, not since he had left home to fulfil his desire to see the world, leaving behind a pubescent sibling who had begged him to take her with him. But common sense and strict parents had buried that wild idea, and Zara had been left in Asia to seek out an education that was normally denied to young women. Now they fell into each other's arms, Strabo muttering about how tall and beautiful she had grown, Zara laughing and crying at the same time. The others stood and stared, even Titius, who was unaccustomed to not being the centre of attention.

Eurycles was first to decide brother and sister should be left to get better acquainted, clicking his fingers to command Niko and Shoeless — the latter properly dressed and shod for once — to follow with the chest. Titius snapped out of his bewilderment and ordered his man to take charge of the messages, but both men found themselves confronted by a small, energetic child.

Frowning at Titius, Ratboy said, 'Are you Mark Antony?' He had no weapon, but his fists were clenched. He had seen Mark Antony from a distance when Lachares was murdered, but to his young mind all Roman officers looked alike. 'Are you?' His young face was now dark with rage.

Titius had no respect for women and less for children. He brushed Ratboy aside with the back of his hand, causing the lad to stumble, and suddenly found himself confronted by three Greek sailors.

'Apologise,' said Eurycles, his face inches from Titius's. The Roman already had a hand on the hilt of his gladius, as did his companion.

'Do you know who I am?' This was the sort of thing a Roman officer would say without thinking.

'No,' replied Eurycles, refusing to be intimidated. 'I don't know who you are, and I really don't care. Now apologise to the boy.'

Titius gave his gladius blade a hand's breadth of daylight. Niko and Shoeless closed ranks beside Eurycles. The air crackled with tension. Three unarmed Spartans and two Romans. And a child spoiling for a fight. All around, dockside workers and slaves stopped what they were doing and gathered closer to what they thought might be an entertaining distraction. But it was Zara who broke the spell.

'Wait,' she said. 'I will show you to the *principia*.'

Eurycles did not know what the *principia* was but guessed it would be some kind of headquarters. Without releasing the Roman's gaze, he said, 'Just as soon as this man apologises to the boy.'

'Marcus Titius is not the type of person to apologise for anything,' said Zara.

Hearing the name of one of the message recipients, Eurycles took a step back. He thought fast and saw an opportunity to avoid a fight.

'So you are Titius? One of the messages I have is for you, as it happens. Another is for your uncle, Plancus. You shall have both when you apologise.'

The effect was instantaneous. Anger and confusion raged on Titius's face, his mouth opening and closing. No apology, just what sounded like 'filthy Greeks'. Eurycles turned to Zara, who still had an arm around her brother's waist.

'Lady, we thank you,' said Eurycles. 'Please lead on.'

'This way,' she said brightly before Titius could react.

The small party followed her and Strabo at a brisk pace past a disappointed crowd, dodging slaves, donkeys, carts and piles of grain sacks and dried food supplies. Scavenging doves and seabirds scattered before them. Eurycles looked back to see Titius and his man following, irresistibly drawn by the promise of word from Rome.

Behind them, to the southwest beyond the harbour mole, the skies were darkening. The Greeks sensed this, knowing that Notos, the god of the south wind, had drawn a hard, stark line across the horizon and would keep them in Samos far longer than Eurycles had intended. The giant ships of Mark Antony and the Egyptian queen could take their chances, but Greek sailors knew better. In normal circumstances, a few days sheltering on Samos would be no hardship for *Hera*'s crew. But Eurycles felt a weight on his shoulders again.

He would be sharing the island with his father's killer.

CHAPTER SIX

The *principia* heaved like a market in uniform. Romans love to wear armour and even the lower ranks, messengers and clerks did their best to look important. To Eurycles, it appeared at first sight to be disorganised, yet everyone in the vast hall seemed to have a purpose, whether hunched over checklists or dashing out of the building, clutching orders for the commanders, quartermasters and centurions in the port. These dodged not only the crowds but also ancient pillars and an imposing statue of Pythagoras as they went about their respective missions. The noise was like putting your head in a beehive, the heat heightening malodorous air. Pigeons cowered in roof and cornice clefts, indignant at the intrusion.

'Welcome to the *principia*,' smiled Zara.

'Worse than the *curia*,' said Strabo, looking uncomfortable.

'Where's Mark Antony?' squeaked Ratboy, jumping energetically in an attempt to see across the crowds. A slap from Eurycles and an angry glare was momentarily calming.

'We should find Publicola,' said Zara. Eurycles remembered a warning from just a few days earlier, concerning Lucius Gellius Publicola. *If you meet him, run the other way or kill him.* He doubted this would be a good place to assassinate one of Mark Antony's commanders. And he couldn't turn and run. Trust the Fates and try to keep out of trouble.

They fought through the crowd, Eurycles conscious that he was about to meet an incestuous murderer and somewhere behind him was Titius, an abhorrent Roman who wouldn't hesitate to push a sharp gladius between his ribs.

At first sight, Publicola didn't appear to be the type to have seduced his stepmother and conspired to murder several Republican dignitaries. Though rugged, his features were unremarkable and he carried surplus weight around the midriff, indicating a life of excess. The clue was in his eyes, too small and lacking any hint of emotion, coldly indifferent. He was surrounded by attendants who were making piles of scrawled vellum orders. These were weighted with stones on a table, ready for dispatch by runners who queued eagerly. There were probably twenty servants awaiting orders. Zara stretched on tiptoe and waved. Men always noticed a woman in a man's world, and Publicola was no exception. He casually waved aside the waiting messengers and beckoned.

'What does Cleopatra's slave girl want?'

Zara ignored the slight. 'Letters from Rome.' She used as few words as possible.

'For whom?'

'Mark Antony.'

The look in Publicola's eye said everything: he would like to read them first. 'Bring them.'

Eurycles moved closer to the table and indicated that Niko and Shoeless should place the box on the floor, not on the table. He bent to open it, trying not to make eye-contact with Publicola, who was studying him intently.

'And who are you?'

'Just a merchant from Taenarum.' Eurycles still refused to make eye-contact, but hesitated as if sorting through a chest of treasure. 'I was contracted to deliver these messages.'

'I haven't got all day. Hand them over.'

Eurycles pulled out the first scroll case, noticed that it was addressed to Plancus and tossed it back. Publicola was now holding out a hand with a sigh and an impatient look on his face that suggested there were more drastic ways of dealing with impertinent Greeks. The first sealed message for Mark Antony was placed in Publicola's hand. Then another, then all but two of the cylinders. Publicola placed them on the table and studied them as if they were scorpions. He clearly wanted to open them but instead leaned forward and looked down into the strongbox that contained two remaining messages.

'And these? Hand them over.'

Eurycles wished he had been more circumspect. Agrippa had been clear that these two messages should be placed in the hands of Plancus and Titius and no other. Instructions for defectors, the evidence of betrayal right there within the two leather cases. He looked around and saw Titius hanging back beyond the throng, a look of horror on his face. All he had to do was hand them to Publicola and there would be one less obnoxious Roman to worry about. And his uncle Plancus, who was probably equally contemptible.

He would have refused to hand them over, but he didn't have to because Mark Antony himself made an entrance at that very moment; all attention was deflected from what the two remaining messages might contain. Everyone in the hall fell silent. Eurycles could have guessed at the newcomer's identity from his flamboyant toga and haughty Roman expression, but Zara leaned close and whispered, 'Antony.' He felt his gut tighten and instinctively his hand moved to his hip, reaching for the dagger that wasn't there.

Ratboy was hopping again. 'Is that him? Is that him?' Eurycles grasped Ratboy by the collar and twisted, drawing him close as the child choked. He didn't doubt the boy would sprint across the room to accost the famous general, now an enemy of Rome. 'If you move or make a sound, I will throw you into the harbour with your feet tied to a rock,' he hissed.

Ratboy seemed to control his bloodlust. The boy knew Eurycles wouldn't drown him, but he respected the merchant seaman enough to obey the command.

For a moment it seemed as if Mark Antony would pass them by, but Publicola hailed him. 'Messages for you, Marcus, from Rome apparently.'

Antony gave a weak smile, his bloodshot eyes betraying a love-hate relationship with the wine cup. 'Rome, eh? Full surrender, no doubt. I expect you've read them already, Lucius?'

Publicola feigned shock. 'Of course not. They've just arrived. They were brought by these Greeks.'

That was the moment when Eurycles locked eyes with his father's killer. He felt his gorge constrict, anger and hate rising irrepressibly. Eyes cold, he forced himself to smile. Perhaps Mark Antony would mistake the look for lowly Greek trepidation in the presence of greatness. He was lost for words, not trusting himself to remain calm. But Antony seemed not to consider the messengers worthy of scrutiny. He merely shrugged, his gaze lingering briefly on Zara before turning back to Publicola.

'Have them delivered to my palace,' he said. 'I shall adopt a reclining position and allow the Senate to entertain me at my leisure.' He turned to leave, then looked back. 'If replies are expected, my secretary will bring them tomorrow.'

Publicola saluted and set about organising the delivery. The two messages, for Plancus and Titius, had momentarily been forgotten.

Zara leaned close to Eurycles. 'I think you probably want to leave?' Eurycles nodded subtly. 'Follow me.' With the majesty of a queen's handmaiden, she turned, parting the throng of open-mouthed messengers like a warship under sail, her brother Strabo beside her. The small party of Greeks followed eagerly, two of them carrying a chest that now contained just two messages. Ratboy puffed out his chest as if he were the most important person in the *principia*. They walked straight past a bewildered Titius, who made to stop them but, for once, found his authority and the power of his uniform ignored. He followed them, his face like thunder.

Outside, away from the crowds, Eurycles ordered Niko and Shoeless to put down the chest and turned to face the approaching Titius. 'Where is your uncle, this Lucius Munatius Plancus?'

Titius scowled, then realised he should co-operate. 'At his villa, writing orders for his men.'

'I fear we are to spend time together, you and your uncle and my noble crew.'

'How do you know this?' said Titius, suspicion showing on his face that this lowlife knew more than he should.

'Never mind that. All will become clear.' He indicated to Niko to open the chest and in a flash Ratboy reached in to gather up the two sealed cylinders. Eurycles smiled to himself. Having the most junior member of his crew hand over the messages would not be lost on the pompous Roman.

Zara watched, intrigued. Titius seemed confused, no doubt realising that he should keep his mouth shut in front of Cleopatra's handmaiden. Eurycles waved Ratboy forward.

'Take these to your uncle and consider your replies,' he said. Ratboy handed them over with a mock bow. 'Take your time and bring your replies to my ship tomorrow.'

'Which ship is that?' The Roman's huff and puff seemed to have dissipated at last.

'The one that isn't Roman or Egyptian. You can't miss it. It's crewed by filthy Greeks.'

CHAPTER SEVEN

Zara took Strabo to the Egyptian quarter so they could become reacquainted, Eurycles went in search of the baths, and *Hera*'s crew frolicked in a cleaner part of the harbour waters.

Dawn the next day was as unpleasant as the Greek seamen had expected. Strong winds drove stinging rain mixed with salty spray off the Aegean, bringing a temporary halt to the exodus of Mark Antony's fleet.

Eurycles and Myron huddled in a drier part of the ship, discussing rotas for allowing the crew ashore and provisioning for a return journey that could be some days off if the weather didn't break. *Hera* rocked and strained against her stern-on moorings, bigger vessels on either side bruising her flanks.

Strabo hailed them from the quayside. He had changed his clothes for more practical *braccae*, a shirt and a leather jerkin but still managed to look bedraggled, his hair slicked by rain and his beard dripping. He climbed aboard clumsily, muttering his preference for solid ground. A bulging leather satchel didn't make the exercise any easier. He collapsed in a heap next to Eurycles and Myron, making even new clothes look untidy.

'And how's life in the Egyptian court?' Eurycles asked cheekily.

'Drier than here,' Strabo replied, opening the satchel to reveal a flagon of exotic design. He handed it to Eurycles. 'I can vouch for the contents; it's distilled from dates, I'm told, but go carefully.'

Eurycles pulled the stopper and took a mouthful, choking on the warming fire. He passed it to Myron, who was more circumspect and didn't choke, but smiled with appreciation.

Strabo recounted the pleasures of an evening with his sister in what sounded like some kind of Alexandrian community transplanted onto Samos. The writer inside him rambled on about Egyptian customs and beliefs and his intention to explore the Nile from Alexandria to Nubia. When Eurycles yawned and Myron looked vacant, he got to the point.

'My sister wants to talk to you in private,' he said, looking at Eurycles.

'What about?'

'If I told you that, it wouldn't be private.'

'Come, Strabo, you can talk openly in front of Myron.'

Strabo looked at Myron. 'No offence, but Zara made me promise to tell no one other than Eurycles here.'

Myron shrugged and began to rise, but Strabo reached out a hand to restrain him.

'Actually, Zara made me promise not to mention anything and to take Eurycles to her, alone.'

'No matter,' said Myron. 'I have duties here, and I need to organise the crew to keep them busy while we're in this port. You two can go off on your secret mission. Don't mind me.'

As he spoke, they heard a rustling nearby.

'You can come out now, Ratboy,' called Eurycles.

A head poked up from behind the sail storage area. Ratboy's wide grin revealed his crooked teeth. His hiding place had been open to the rain, and he was more than a little damp, though undeterred in his mission to know everything that was going on.

'I'm coming too,' he said, as if it were his right.

Myron laughed. 'And how will you manage that, when your duty today is to scrub the rowing benches?'

Sometimes the most private places are in full view. Zara was waiting for Eurycles and Strabo in what seemed to be a cross between a traders' bazaar and a huge tavern, Egyptian street life brought to an island off Asia Minor. Vast canopies stretched across a wide street, keeping the rain at bay. Beneath these, a hundred well-to-do Egyptians sat at tables where they were served from the many braziers at which servants cooked aromatic dishes. A weak sun was barely up yet there was the cacophony of animated discussions and heated debate about the day's tasks. Eurycles had been to Alexandria only once in his life, trading cloth and delivering a Corinthian diplomat, so the spicy aromas and colourful, noisy crowds brought back a fond memory. Privacy was assured.

Zara shooed away the small beggar-boys who were hounding Strabo and Eurycles and invited both men to sit at a table that rocked unsteadily on uneven cobbles. She clicked her fingers without looking at any servant, and instantly cups were placed before each of them. A second servant then poured fragrant, milky froth, and a third brought pastries still warm from the ovens. Rainwater dripped from the overhead canopies but miraculously not onto their breakfast.

'This is one good reason why I will go to Egypt,' smiled Strabo, who wasted no time in consuming a honeyed pastry, crumbs settling in his beard like birds gathering in a tree.

Zara placed a hand on his arm with a pleasing jangle of gold bracelets. 'Perhaps I will come with you, but I fear my path is westwards, not south.'

Eurycles found himself admiring her elegant gestures and the light in her eyes. Even when not looking directly at her, he was drawn by her presence and had to force himself not to stare. There was something in her perfect imperfection, her appealing freckles on either side of her strong nose, her olive skin contrasting with such strikingly white teeth. He blushed when he realised she had just asked him where his path lay.

'I … well…' Hating himself for stammering, he took a breath and confessed. 'I really don't know.'

Zara looked into his eyes and his heart missed a beat. 'I think you have been drawn into this awful mess,' she said with a hint of sadness. 'Tell me about your home. Where is it and what do you do there?'

Eurycles began by explaining where Taenarum lay, then rambled about the simple life of a Spartan community, a life at sea, and so on. *Be quiet, Eurycles*, he thought. *She's not interested in all that.* But to her credit, she listened. Strabo, too, seemed intrigued. He found himself wishing one of them would interrupt and became more hesitant.

Then came a moment that changed his life.

She gently laid her hand on his arm. He felt something surge through those long, elegant fingers, through his skin to flesh and blood beneath, where it pulsed through his entire body. A raindrop splashed on the back of her hand, the goddess Amphitrite's approval.

'And your parents?' She spoke softly, as if knowing tragedy lay there.

Eurycles told her about his mother's illness and the injustices of the gods towards her. He then spoke about his father, the courageous trader. He was about to tell her about a greater injustice when he suddenly silenced himself. He was talking too much. Was not this hypnotic woman part of the very regime that had cruelly executed his father?

Zara's hand was still on his arm. She squeezed gently. 'Go on, tell me.'

Afterwards, Eurycles wondered how he had opened his heart to a woman he barely knew. A woman who worked for the Queen of Egypt, who had probably persuaded her lover Mark Antony to execute his father. Had Zara bewitched him? Yet somehow he trusted her. And here was Strabo next to him, making assurances that Zara wouldn't betray him.

There was a moment's silence when his account slowed and then stopped. She squeezed his arm again.

'I know. I was there.'

'What? You saw my father die?'

'Yes,' she said, moving her hand to touch his cheek. 'He was brave. I think the queen expected entertainment for her court, but your father was dignified and strong in the face of such animal behaviour.' She could tell Eurycles was fighting tears. 'His death was not in vain, because many here now question whether the gods have deserted my queen and Mark Antony.'

Eurycles composed himself, then asked bluntly, 'So what will you do?'

'Right now, I do not know, but if you are friends with this Agrippa in Rome as Strabo says, I can help.'

'What do you mean?'

Strabo interjected. 'Mark Antony has been careless. Apparently he left his maps lying around after one of his drunken sessions with Queen Cleopatra.'

'I think I see what you are saying,' said Eurycles. 'You want to be a spy for Rome?' He touched the viper *fibula* pinned on his chest — the badge of Agrippa's spy network.

Zara nodded, sweeping a strand of dark hair from her face. She studied the viper brooch.

'But that is so dangerous,' said Eurycles. 'Have you any idea what Antony would do to you if he found out?'

'I saw what he did to your father. I would be proud to join him in the Underworld if that is my fate, but it isn't. Not yet. And I know where Antony will seek battle with this Caesar in Rome.'

This time, when Eurycles looked into her eyes, he didn't melt. He saw steely determination there, and he knew not only that he could trust her, but also that she could look after herself.

'Tell me about the maps,' he said.

Then Strabo at last justified his involvement in the expedition. His ambition was to be a geographer first and a writer second, creating understanding for the masses of the world they lived in. For the kings, senators and generals, he would record who ruled what and where. Zara said that after gathering troops and ships at Athens, the legions and fleet would move west.

'To invade Italia?' asked Eurycles.

'No,' replied Zara. 'Antony wants to fight in Greece. He has fought there before, with the first Caesar, apparently, and he wants to emulate that triumph. If he defeats Octavian in Greece, Italia will be open to him. And Rome also, of course.'

Strabo leaned forward. 'Octavian will agree to this, if he hasn't already. He would prefer to fight on the edge of Mark Antony's territories and keep war away from his homeland.'

'So where?' Eurycles asked.

Zara made a circling motion as if she was holding a writing stick. 'They have marked rings around the Temple of Apollo — as if this is the god who will give them victory.'

'Where's that?' asked Eurycles.

Strabo showed off his knowledge. 'It's on the west coast at the southern end of a narrow strait leading into a large inland sea called Ambracia. It's famous enough to have all kinds of festivals and games. It would appeal to someone like Antony.'

Zara raised an eyebrow. 'Do they have drinking games at these festivals? Antony would be champion.'

'What interests me more than Apollo's temple,' said Eurycles, 'is this Ambracian Sea. I know it well. There are plenty of sheltered anchorages. You could hide a whole fleet there, and the eastern end is that much closer for Antony's legions to reach overland.' He scratched his chin. 'Except…'

'Except,' interrupted Strabo, 'it would be easy to trap such a fleet if Octavian and Agrippa knew they were there.'

'Precisely. That channel into the gulf is so narrow it would be easy to blockade. You could even chuck rocks at the ships from the shore as they tried to break out.' Eurycles turned to Zara and lowered his voice, not that anyone nearby was listening. 'You realise how valuable this information might be? You're taking a huge risk telling us about it.'

Zara nodded. Her eyes said she was sure.

'You must come with us,' he said. 'Get away from Cleopatra and Antony before they suspect anything.'

She touched his arm again. 'They won't. Why should they? I've been careful. Besides, I've made friends here and I'm not about to sail away with a bunch of filthy Greeks!'

They all laughed and called for something stronger. To all observers, they were just a beautiful Anatolian, her chubby brother and a Greek trader — friends enjoying a morning repast before braving the unseasonal elements to go about their work.

They were so taken up with toasting each other that they did not see the hooded man lurking in the doorway of a nearby bakery. Marcus Titius drew his cloak closer. He had seen enough, and although he had heard nothing of the conversation, he knew how to embellish a story to teach that whore a lesson.

CHAPTER EIGHT

Ratboy didn't like what he was seeing.

He had slipped away from the ship and followed Eurycles and Strabo. He watched them talk and laugh with the beautiful woman and knew full well that all three were good people plunged into a town of bad people. And that nasty Titius fellow was watching them from doorway shadows.

Nobody saw Ratboy, not when he didn't want to be seen. That would work as long as he kept his mouth shut, and right now he was watching and not talking. Watching Titius watching his friends. When people watched other people, they were up to no good. Except for Ratboy, of course — that was his job. All in a good cause.

So when the small Roman who had disguised himself with a hooded cloak sneaked away, he followed. There was no need to warn Eurycles and the others; he would deal with it all by himself. He left them to their laughing and chatting. This was his duty and no one else's.

He followed Titius down a side alley, just far enough behind not to be noticed, dodging fat women with billowing aprons sweeping damp streets outside their doors. But he forgot to watch his back.

He turned instinctively when he felt the tap on his shoulder. He had just enough time to register the face of a boy larger than himself before the push on his chest. Then he was falling backwards, tripping over a strategically placed foot and sprawling onto his back. He sprung back to his feet with his fists raised to fight before realising that there were too many opponents. All four laughed at him.

'Go on, then. Fight if you want — it won't take long.'

The eldest boy thrust his face close to Ratboy's. The dark, wispy hairs on his chin indicated that he was older by maybe a couple of years, and his black, narrowed eyes and hard-set lips suggested he knew more about surviving. Maybe he even knew a little brutality.

Duty to his friends came first. Ratboy couldn't let Titius get away. He turned to see the hooded Roman turn left at the end of the alley.

'Please let me go,' he said, hating himself for pleading. 'That man is up to no good and —'

Hairy Chin pushed him again. 'What are you going to do? Kill him?' He said this with a sneering laugh.

'If I have to. Him and Mark Antony too.'

That got Hairy Chin's attention. 'So, a little assassin, eh? How many Romans have you killed, little man?'

'Please. I must follow him. He is going to harm my friends and Zara.'

Hairy Chin's reaction to the mention of Zara was fleeting, but it registered. 'We don't care about your friends, but we do care about Zara,' he said. 'Fall in behind us and if you value your life, say nothing and do as we tell you.'

Hairy Chin's three friends were all about the same age, or at least the same height. Ratboy knew better than to protest. He followed them as they dodged the fat women with brooms, turned left and followed Titius who was oblivious to their presence. The Roman made several more turns and approached the double doors of an impressive townhouse. He knocked at the visitor hatch which was instantly swept open. A short conversation took place before the hatch was slammed shut. The five youths watched from a safe distance as the doors opened a few moments later, and Publicola stepped into the street. Ratboy's heart sank. He could think of no worse enemy to Eurycles, save Mark Antony himself, or to Zara for that matter. From what little he had seen of Publicola, Ratboy knew he was the worst kind of Roman officer. Worse even than Titius.

'What's the problem with this man?' Hairy Chin whispered to Ratboy.

'He's a traitor for one, but also he wants to harm Zara.'

'Zara's our friend. She gives us clothes, food and money. That's why we watch over her. We care nothing for either of these two Romans.'

'And she likes my boss,' said Ratboy, adding, 'I like her too.'

The hard look on Hairy Chin's face softened for a moment.

'Give me something that I can use to stop this Titius, short of killing him. Anything.'

'He and his uncle are going to defect.' Ratboy knew he was playing with fire, but he had to prevent a disaster. 'My boss has been sent to take them to Rome.'

Hairy Chin smiled, and his young friends nudged elbows in a conspiratorial way. They clearly didn't like Titius either. 'What's your name?'

'Ratboy.'

'Good name. Mine's Panther. Now, watch and be amazed.'

Panther seemed to shrivel. He set off towards Publicola and Titius, who were engaged in animated discussion. He dragged his right leg behind him and groped ahead as if half blind. As he passed the Romans, he tugged Titius's cloak and said, 'Your men have landed on the west coast. They are ready to attack Mark Antony from the rear at sunset.'

That was all. Then he shuffled off, just another helpless messenger delivering an inopportune message to an unfortunate Roman officer.

The two Romans froze, Publicola staring after Panther. Then he turned to Titius as a look of pure hatred crossed his face.

Titius gathered his cloak and ran for his life.

CHAPTER NINE

The rain eased the next day but the wind was stubborn, now from the south-east, allowing more of the larger ships to set course for Athens. The Egyptian flagship *Antonia* remained moored, the royal passengers not yet ready to depart. This gave Eurycles hope that he could spend more time with Zara before he too sailed for Taenarum with Titius and Plancus, should they ever show up. He was tempted to sail without them if the wind dropped — a temptation he would resist, however unpleasant the thought of several days at sea with two such loathsome characters was. *Hera* strained against her moorings, as if eager to depart without the Romans.

Samos port hesitantly came to life as dawn's weak sunlight winked back from the sodden stone quay. Eurycles stepped ashore and found himself gazing towards Samos town in the hope that he would see Zara striding towards him. Myron brought what was left of Strabo's firewater.

'That will get your mind off whatever is troubling you.'

Eurycles drank and said nothing.

'My guess is that it's a woman,' said Myron.

Eurycles smiled weakly and handed the flagon back, still silent.

'Thought so. Nothing new there. You'll be over it as soon as we're in open seas.'

At last Eurycles spoke. 'This is different.'

Now it was Myron's turn to say nothing. Both men stared along the quayside towards the town. They spotted Strabo, weaving through the gathering crowds of dockers, soldiers and slaves who were shaking off sleep, ready for the day's exertions. He was red-faced and flustered despite the morning's chill, his new clothes crumpled as if he had slept in them. But Strabo hadn't slept at all during the stormy night. He stood before the two men and ran a hand through his unruly hair, whipped by the wind. His mouth opened and closed, as if he couldn't find the right words in what was clearly an emergency.

Myron passed him the flagon. 'Deep breath. Drink, then speak.'

Strabo waved it away. 'It's Zara,' he managed. Eurycles tensed as Strabo continued, 'Publicola's men were looking for her, but Ratboy and some lads found her first.'

'Where is she now?' asked Eurycles.

'Safe, I hope, with the Egyptian queen where Publicola's ruffians aren't welcome. But I worry for her.'

'What did they want with her?'

'Ratboy thinks it was that bastard Titius. They followed him and saw him speaking to Publicola, and we know that if there's one person more dangerous than Titius, it's Publicola.'

Eurycles cursed quietly. 'And Titius feels slighted by Zara. Then what happened?'

'Ratboy says this gang of boys are devoted to Zara, and their leader found a way to divert attention from Zara and land Titius in the mire. Clever lads, it seems. But now this Publicola fellow is hunting my sister *and* Titius.'

'Where's Ratboy now?'

'Shadowing Titius with some of his new friends. It seems he and his uncle are now in a hurry to leave. But it might not take long for Publicola to work out what's going on. You — all of us — could be implicated, and that would mean big trouble.'

Eurycles turned to Myron and ordered him to prepare to set sail. He hated himself for thinking that he could leave Zara to the mercy of uncouth Romans, but he knew he must. Agrippa had sent him to extract two defectors and he would keep his word, and perhaps the Egyptian queen would keep her safe. He vowed he would find Zara wherever the Fates took her, perhaps when this power struggle was finally settled. He put a hand on Strabo's shoulder.

'You stay on the ship, ready to leave as soon as Titius and Plancus turn up.'

Strabo shook his head. 'I'm not leaving. How could I? I have found my little sister after so many years, and now she is in danger.'

'But Agrippa is expecting you…'

'Neither Agrippa nor Octavian own me. But they trust me. I am staying.' A commotion on the edge of Samos town momentarily distracted them. 'That could be Titius and Plancus,' said Strabo. 'No time for fond farewells, I fear.'

Eurycles reached into a pocket where he kept the spare viper brooch that Agrippa had given him. 'I know you are a friend, Strabo, and I am sure we will meet again one day soon. But forgive me for saying that I yearn to see your sister too. Take this to her.' Strabo took it. He knew what it meant: it was a secret bond between people who stood for a better world. Eurycles touched his own *fibula* brooch. 'Tell her I will wear mine until I find her.'

Strabo nodded, embraced Eurycles as a brother, and melted into the quayside crowd.

Myron, noticing that Eurycles was strangely distracted, sent Niko and Shoeless to look for the Roman passengers. 'And don't come back without Ratboy,' he called after them. He then looked across the harbour anchorage and beyond to frenzied seas, and wondered what sacrifice Poseidon would demand if *Hera* and her crew were to survive this day.

Ratboy watched from behind a supply cart and cursed. Crouching next to him, Panther laughed. Titius and Plancus led a column of slaves, carrying their luggage. At least they weren't dressed in ceremonial uniform, although their fine cloaks and heavy boots were hardly rank and file attire. Titius was small and arrogant, his uncle dragging his left foot. It was painfully obvious who they were, if anyone cared to look closely.

And someone was looking.

Panther tapped Ratboy's shoulder and pointed to group of armed soldiers, whose leader was sizing up the column headed by two nobles making for the moored ships. The wind was whistling through the cart's disjointed slats. Harnessed to it, a pair of mules hung their heads forlornly. One of them defecated. Panther raised his voice above the wind and dockside clamour.

'By the time you count to ten, those soldiers will have other things on their minds,' he said. 'Then you can lead those Roman pricks to your ship.'

He slipped away.

Ratboy was using his fingers to count when he felt another tap on his shoulder.

'Call that a hiding place?' said Shoeless. Niko was weighing up the dockside scene.

'If you're worried about those soldiers, they'll be gone soon,' said Ratboy. 'Just watch.'

'I'm more worried about that luggage,' said Niko. 'We'll have to lose the whole lot if we're going to get away safely.'

There was an angry shout from the soldiers' leader, clutching at his knee. Then there was a bright ringing sound as a small stone pinged off his helmet. The soldiers looked around but couldn't see their assailants. Then more stones flew, clearly slingshots, from several directions at once. The soldiers lost interest in the two Romans they had been shadowing, and when Panther stood up from his hiding place, waving cheekily, they gave chase.

'You lead the Romans to the ship,' Niko said to Ratboy. 'We'll deal with the luggage slaves.'

Ratboy sprinted up to Titius and Plancus, who were looking around in confusion.

'Sirs, this way, please.'

'Who are you?' Plancus said, looking down his nose at the boy.

'I am to lead you to your ship.' He tugged at Plancus's hem. The old man slapped his hand away, but Titius knew who Ratboy was and reassured his uncle.

Niko and Shoeless had slipped past them and took command of the slave column. This alarmed Titius, who thought the two sailors were thieves.

'You go on ahead,' said Niko. 'We'll follow.' He had no intention of following with such pointless baggage and knew exactly what he going to do with it. His preference was to throw it into the harbour, but there were plenty of people who needed clothing and luxuries, the slaves themselves chief among them.

Ratboy led the two Romans to *Hera*. Moored stern-to-quay, she was now held by just one line while crew members used boat hooks to hold her position. Her stern was grinding solidly on stone as the wind rocked her. A gangplank rose from the quay to the command platform, where a section of railing had been removed. Simple enough for seasoned sailors — not so for Roman nobility.

Ratboy ushered them to the precarious gangplank. It slid alarmingly as the ship heaved. Eurycles himself held out a hand for the older man, who protested vehemently while Titius looked around for the luggage bearers. They were nowhere to be seen. But what was now in evidence was more soldiers systematically working their way along the quay, no doubt looking for the fugitive defectors. Publicola's men.

Plancus stumbled aboard and Ratboy pushed Titius in the back, using more aggression than was necessary, forcing him to embark. As he stumbled onto a lowly Greek trading ship, he yelled venomous curses at anyone within hearing, probably regretting that he had now thrown in his lot with Octavian and there was no going back. He thrashed wildly at Ratboy, who had followed him, but his blows were easily dodged.

The soldiers were now just fifty paces away, and Publicola himself led them.

Eurycles ordered that the gangplank be raised and summoned archers to the stern — four of them. He saw Niko and Shoeless sprinting towards *Hera* just as it dawned on Publicola which ship was about to depart with their quarry on board. He saw the men running and made the correct assumption that they were part of the conspiracy. At his command, the soldiers formed up and drew short swords just as a hail of slingshots hurtled towards them, maiming with sickening effect. Publicola himself, helmetless, was felled by a stone fired by a boy a third of his age. Later, he would tell anyone willing to listen how he had fought a barbarian horde and survived with just a broken nose.

Niko and Shoeless did not break stride and leapt aboard as Myron ordered, 'Let go aft!' *Hera* leapt to freedom. Her mainsail was hoisted even before she had cleared the neighbouring vessels. Her rowers were ready, should they be needed. She heeled before the south-westerly on her port beam as her sail filled, Niko and Shoeless holding her course with twin steering rudders as she surged towards the harbour mouth.

Ratboy stood in the stern and saluted four boys on the quayside, their slings now slack by their sides. The archers weren't needed. By the time Publicola had recovered sufficiently to order a chase, *Hera* had long gone. She rounded the breakwater and bucked and plunged on rough seas that at times threatened to swallow her. But she was not awed by Poseidon's power, and the winds were fair as she ploughed onwards towards Taenarum.

By this time, the two angry Romans on board were too sick to care that their baggage had been left behind.

CHAPTER TEN

Marcus Vipsanius Agrippa's second visit to Taenarum was completely different to his first. This time he came with a fleet of ten ships, three triremes crewed by seasoned marines and seven larger transporters. His triremes were armed with deadly *harpax* weapons that could grapple enemy shipping and draw them to close quarters for boarding. Lately he had adapted the weapons to be able to fire flaming bolts that could pierce a ship's flank, setting infernos below decks that would cause panic, mayhem and an agonising death for hapless rowers.

There were more of the fearsome *ballistae* stored on one of the transporter ships, a gift for Eurycles to install on his Greek *liburnians*. But more importantly there was also the gift of gold and men — soldiers and engineers — who were to secure the town and the port for Rome. This was because Taenarum, the southernmost port of the Peloponnesus peninsula, commanded the shipping supply line from the East to the Ionian Sea between Greece and Italia. Mark Antony's fleet would doubtless pass this way one day soon, as would his supply ships coming up from Egypt's grain stores. A sleepy trading port was about to have enormous strategic importance thrust upon it.

Hera had returned to Taenarum just one day earlier, and Eurycles was doing his best to avoid the whining complaints of Titius and the grumbling of his uncle, Plancus. He was enjoying an anonymous afternoon alone in a backstreet tavern, where no one could find him. Except Ratboy, of course, who suddenly appeared unannounced as rats do.

'Ships approaching,' said Ratboy, proud to be first to break the news to Taenarum's de facto ruler.

Eurycles was too exhausted to worry. 'How many?' When Ratboy held up both hands, fingers extended, he rightly assumed ten. 'Who are they?'

'Myron says they are flying Rome's colours.'

Eurycles hauled himself to his feet, nodded to the host, dropped over-generous payment on the table, and went to see for himself. Coloured pennants meant nothing. They could be Roman, Egyptian, traders, or even pirates. And ten ships would be too much for Taenarum's insignificant fleet, inadequate forces and limited hospitality.

He joined Myron at the harbour. Niko and Shoeless were with him, the latter fully clothed but barefoot. Nine ships stood off beyond the breakwater, while a tenth made its way into the harbour.

'Roman,' said Myron. 'But why so many?'

'My guess is it's Agrippa,' said Eurycles, 'coming for Titius and Plancus.' He sent Ratboy to find the two Romans, then said to Myron, 'I'll be glad to see the back of them.'

The others laughed; the journey home had been treacherous enough without the sour behaviour of the so-called noblemen — particularly Titius, who between bouts of seasickness had treated *Hera*'s crew with utter contempt.

It was indeed Agrippa who came to Taenarum on calm seas that sparkled in crisp winter sunshine, with barely a breeze to trouble his anchored fleet. He hailed them from the trireme's bows as the ship approached, seeking space to dock among the port's ramshackle fishing boats. This time, there no mistaking the man's power. He was dressed in full ceremonial armour, clutching a plumed helmet with his left hand. Weak sunlight reflected from silver-inlaid breastplate.

By now a crowd had gathered on the quayside. Among them, women and children pointed and chattered while the men looked on solemnly, hoping they would not be expected to fight to protect their homes and their livelihoods. Myron picked out several of the fishermen whose boats crowded the best moorings and ordered them to make room for the approaching warship. They obliged. The Roman navy had a reputation for bullying smaller vessels.

As the trireme docked, Titius came running, Plancus limping after him. They were wearing lowly Greek attire, having ordered an innkeeper's wife to launder their finery, which had suffered during the stormy days at sea. Agrippa stepped ashore alone. In other circumstances this would have been a foolish gesture, but his reputation preceded him. The crowd gave him respectful space. Titius, doing his best to overcome the embarrassment of meeting his superior while dressed so inadequately, pushed past Eurycles to salute Agrippa, who simply gave a wry smile. Eurycles read the expression correctly: scorn. Plancus, a man used to reading the signs in other men, unlike his nephew, chose to remain silent. Titius began a tirade of complaints about 'these filthy Greeks', pointing an accusing finger at Eurycles. Spittle formed on his thin lips as his eyes flashed venomously.

Agrippa heard him out. Ratboy sniggered when Titius's rant slowed. Those nearest waited in silence as the ill-dressed Roman ran out of words and thrust out his jaw, like a tavern brawler challenging a rival. Agrippa's slight was deafening. He simply reached out his left arm to Eurycles, placing it respectfully on the Spartan's shoulder while clasping right arm to right arm in the traditional Roman greeting.

'Thank you, Eurycles,' he smiled, 'and my thanks to your noble crew.'

Titius looked as though he had been punched in the throat.

Eventually, Agrippa turned to Titius and Plancus. 'Gentlemen, Caesar Octavian sends his greetings and his gratitude to you both. He has ordered that you be well looked after and afforded comfortable passage to Brundisium where he will meet you in person to accompany you to Rome. Your friends in the Senate are eager to welcome you home and hear of your, ah, *adventures* with Mark Antony. But first, we have business here in Taenarum, and I have much to discuss with my good friend Eurycles.'

At that, the onlookers turned to one another to debate what they had just heard and begin the joyful task of spreading the day's gossip. Agrippa took the opportunity to lean close to Eurycles.

'Somewhere secluded, I think. We have much to discuss.'

It was the map that excited Agrippa. The one that Zara had seen, indicating Mark Antony's chosen arena of war to decide the world's future.

Yes, he wanted to know about ship numbers, Antony's intentions, his mood, what the Egyptian queen was thinking, movements of legions. And where was Strabo? Eurycles could answer few of these questions. But he told the Roman about Zara, and Agrippa knew immediately that his man had lost his heart to the woman and would not hesitate to go back into the lion's den to win her back. He devoured Eurycles' description of the Ambracian gulf and the Temple of Apollo at Actium.

'You know this place?' Agrippa asked.

Eurycles nodded. They ate honeyed figs and sipped local wine in the same tavern where they had first discussed world affairs on Agrippa's first visit.

'Do you want another chance to destroy Antony?'

This time, Eurycles hesitated.

'Look,' Agrippa continued, seeing the doubt and understanding his reluctance to leave Taenarum to a horde of Roman soldiers. 'You know the area well, and you are Greek. You will be able to come and go without suspicion. Find Strabo and this woman — Zara? — and report back what you see and hear.'

Eurycles said nothing, the silence pregnant with his fears for the small community under his care.

'I promise you, Eurycles, my man Rufus is no tyrant and he will govern well. Besides, he was brought up among Greeks and knows your customs. Your people will be looked after and enriched by this garrison. You can judge for yourself when you meet him to lay down some firm rules. Taenarum will become wealthy and prosperous overnight.'

'Not if Mark Antony wants it back. What happens then?'

'We have, what, perhaps half a year, maybe more, during which time we will make the harbour impregnable with a mighty chain across the entrance and fortify the town so that it is impregnable. But you, Eurycles, you have a mission of your own. Am I not right?'

And Eurycles knew he would relent. He had to see the bigger picture. The world was going to change, and Taenarum would change with it. If he could trust this Rufus, he would follow his heart and help Agrippa win his war, find Zara, and do his best to kill Antony. For his father. For Lachares.

'I'll do it,' he said. 'But I bring my own men.'

The old fishing boat had been repaired and plugged more times than her owner, old Castor whose gnarled face hid behind a forest of brittle beard, could recall. But she was deep-keeled and rode waves as well as any.

'She'll do,' said Agrippa. He put an arm around the old fisherman's shoulders. 'How much?'

'Not for sale,' Castor growled. He knew nothing beyond supplying a daily catch of eels, bass, mullet and octopus. It was all he had done since before he could remember, like his father before him. He would die in that boat, preferably at sea where no one, not his nagging wife, his chattering daughters nor his many grandchildren, could bother his spirit with endless wailing and a chest-beating funeral procession.

While Agrippa explained an alternative involving enough gold to build a new boat, even a fleet of them if he so desired, Eurycles and Myron inspected the vessel that was to provide a cover story to enable them to visit the shores around Actium without arousing suspicion. It was a sound plan. Scores of fishing boats plied their trade all around Peloponnesus and the western Greek coast; Mark Antony's guards and scouts wouldn't give the leaky old tub a second glance. Large enough to carry six men, possibly more, each rotating rowing, rigging and steering duties, with room for storage of nets, hooked lines and baskets for the catch — or weapons and light armour. *Hera* would tow her to some secluded cove, where she would begin her spying mission around the island of Leukas and the Ambracian Gulf where Mark Antony and Caesar Octavian would clash — if their intelligence was correct.

'Needs a new sail,' said Myron, eyeing the threadbare cloth furled around a lateen-style boom. 'And these ropes are all rotten.'

'Easily fixed,' said Eurycles, who was warming to the prospect of such a mission.

He glanced over to where Castor was peering into a large purse that Agrippa held open. Inside, there was more gold coin than the old man could have dreamt possible.

'I think the tub is ours,' he said. 'Now, what do you think of Agrippa's other crazy idea?'

Agrippa revelled in his role as Caesar's spymaster. He had set up a spy ring of trusted vipers that stretched from Rome to Gaul in the West and from Parthia to Judea in the East. Coded messages took weeks to reach him by land or sea, but this time it would be different.

His spy in Mark Antony's camp would be a priest. The Temple of Apollo at Actium was a hotbed of mad prophets, seers and holy men, all proclaiming their nonsense to anyone who would listen. And when Agrippa revealed his plan, Eurycles immediately knew the ideal person to take on such a role.

'A wild hairy man who talks gibberish?'

'Yes,' agreed Agrippa. 'The craziest you've got.'

'A fearless hermit sort of man?'

'Yes.'

'But who's capable with a sword should that be necessary?'

'Yes.'

So Eurycles called for Shoeless Luka and promoted him to Chief Priest at the Temple of Apollo. Shoeless looked at him askance, an eyebrow raised, and muttered a curse that would embarrass any holy man.

'You want me to do *what* exactly?'

So Agrippa and Eurycles told him everything and Shoeless did what Shoeless always did. He rubbed his hands together, looked to the heavens as if he could see Apollo's chariot crossing the firmament, and gave his decision.

'Recognition at last. Lead me on!'

He danced a few barefoot steps, chanting incomprehensibly about being a holy man, then stopped suddenly and looked from Eurycles to Agrippa and back again.

'I'll need an altar boy to help me with all those sacrifices.'

Eurycles didn't hesitate. 'You can have Ratboy. But sacrifice animals only, mind. Unless you can get your bloody hands on Mark Antony.'

Shoeless went to find Ratboy and steal a priest's clothes, preferably robes with enough folds to conceal a knife or two.

This was going to be fun.

PART TWO: SACRIFICE

CHAPTER ELEVEN

Actium, West Coast of Greece, Summer 31 BC

The gods of war did not favour Mark Antony.

Bad enough that Plancus, now back in Rome, had put his will into the hands of Octavian, who had stirred up the senate against him and his Egyptian queen. Bad also that the upstart Agrippa had taken the key strongholds of Corcyra, Methone, Petrae and Taenarum, cutting off supply lines and keeping his fleet of magnificent ships hog-tied in this god-awful gulf like caged wild animals. Bad enough that, on land, his cavalry had been beaten back by that obnoxious traitor Titius and his legions forced to retire to a new camp at Actium.

Worse, there was nowhere to escape the mosquitoes and biting insects that swarmed out of endless swamps, causing sickness and hallucinatory fevers that were aggravated by hunger and starvation and the relentless summer heat. Antony felt like a loser already, despite his superior troop numbers and his reputation for heroic leadership, however dented by failures in Parthia. And there were all those deserters, not just Titius and Plancus, but client kings and their armies, and Roman nobles who conveniently forgot their oaths that had been forged in Asian blood.

'I'm pissing into the wind,' he told Cleopatra, collapsing into soft cushions under her tent's vast canopy at the centre of the Egyptian camp. He picked up a small, dull-looking cake, inspected it, and returned it to its golden platter in disgust.

Cleopatra VII Philopator paid him no attention. She was studying the manifests of gold, silver and coin that bankrolled this increasingly aimless war. She traced the rows of figures with a delicate finger bearing a large carnelian clasped by finely worked gold. She wore an ankle-length sheath dress fringed with gold and sky blue to emphasise the curves of her hips and midriff, which were still full from bearing four children. Gold and silver bracelets made music with every slight movement, driving Antony wild with desire. Her dark hair had been braided with silver thread in the Asian style by her handmaiden, Zara, who now sat patiently beside her, ready to pass over the next set of figures prepared by the royal accountants.

'I said, I'm pissing into the wind,' repeated Antony.

Cleopatra didn't bother to look up. 'Piss in another direction then.'

Zara tried and failed to suppress a snigger. She bit her lip when Antony glared at her, cursing inwardly at her folly. She had been marked as a subversive by his general Publicola and was now confined to the queen's camp, where no Roman could lay a hand on her. Not that she wanted to venture outside into a world of disease, starvation and dwindling morale. She knew the climax to this sorry affair was close at hand and was privy to her mistress's impatience with her lover and her secret desire to return to Egypt and her beloved children.

Mark Antony was clearly annoyed. The kohl around his eyes made his mood seem darker. Zara knew his drinking had worsened with every desertion and although the day was barely two hours old, she knew it fuelled a foul temper that could erupt over the smallest matter.

'And what direction would the Queen of Egypt suggest?' He almost spat the words.

Cleopatra looked up. Her violet eyes challenged her lover. 'You know the answer to that.'

'We still have more legions than Octavian, and my generals beg me to mobilise.'

'You would lose,' said Cleopatra calmly. 'Your men are sick and hungry, while Octavian's are well fed with lavish supplies that arrive daily from Italia. He is organised, you are not.'

Antony changed his mind about the cake. He took a bite and his nose wrinkled at its drabness. All this Egyptian wealth and no decent food to show for it.

'I know what you're thinking,' he said, softening. 'But Octavian has more ships than we have.'

'Ours are bigger. They carry more men. They have bigger towers for archers and slingers. Our *ballistae* throw more fire than Octavian could imagine. That's where you can defeat him.'

Just for a moment, Antony registered the word 'you' in place of 'we'. He dismissed it as an irrelevant slip. Her ships were enormous sea-borne fortresses, bristling with firepower. Octavian's were tiny in comparison, though lighter and faster. Cleopatra was right — hares may be quick, but foxes still eat them. Yet the great Mark Antony, general to the all-conquering Julius Caesar, former Triumvir and now ruler of the Eastern provinces, was not a man to give in easily.

He rose to leave. 'Romans fight on land, not at sea.'

Zara watched Mark Antony's broad shoulders leave the royal tent and breathed out, relieved to no longer be in the presence of a ruthless murderer. Stubborn he may be, but she and the queen both knew he would fight this war at sea, and he would likely be defeated. She had heard much of this Agrippa from Eurycles — how he had built a navy to crush the Sicilian pirates and with that victory had given his captains valuable experience, whereas Mark Antony had none.

But she also knew why Cleopatra was pushing for this now, before the summer turned to stormy autumn and the seas became too unpredictable. Her queen had confided in her, for she had her trust. Cleopatra would take the first opportunity to flee from this awful place and fight her battles somewhere else.

The image of Eurycles' youthful face was as strong in her mind and now, just for a moment, she dwelled on those mischievous eyes and the wide grin whenever he thought he had said something amusing. Where was he now? Probably looking after his people in Taenarum, sensibly keeping away from this stinking cauldron of war and pestilence.

Cleopatra handed her stack of accounts to Zara and retired to her private quarters, calling for her ablution slaves. Alone in the tent's reception room, Zara hummed to herself as she opened one of the queen's storage chests at the back of the room. She was placing the documents in it when she heard a familiar sound.

'Psst.'

She looked around and saw nothing, but she knew who it was. 'Panther?'

'Over here.'

The youth always lived up to his name with his talent for appearing unannounced beside her in the camp's market or in a makeshift officers' tavern, or springing from behind a soldier's tent, sometimes with his equally elusive friends.

She followed the sound of his voice and saw movement behind a small mountain of colourful material awaiting the attention of the court's seamstresses. Panther's grinning face appeared.

'Fool, you'll be crucified if you're found here,' Zara chided.

'Oh, the queen doesn't mind. She trusts me.'

'You've spoken to her?'

'Of course. She pays well for information, unlike you,' said Panther with a wink.

'You heard?'

'Oh yes. That Mark Antony is a liar. He wants to flee on his ships as much as the queen does.'

'Panther! Do you eavesdrop on everyone? That's so risky…'

'You ought to hear what they say about the queen. They hate her. They blame her for everything that's going wrong.'

Zara knew this but had kept quiet. Cleopatra probably knew it too. She had an uneasy feeling that this wouldn't end well and regretted not taking her chance to get away with Eurycles. She would find her brother, Strabo; he would know what to do, if he could interrupt his writing for long enough to listen.

She suddenly realised Panther was still talking, telling her something about a temple.

'You should meet him… I will take you there…'

'Sorry, Panther, I was miles away. What are you trying to tell me?'

'The new priest at Apollo's Temple. You've met him before. He doesn't wear shoes.'

CHAPTER TWELVE

The cavernous Temple of Apollo thrummed to the rural music of pipes and drums. Crowds pressed to watch naked, oiled wrestlers grappling each other, the needy and desperate bringing protesting chickens and goats to the sacrificial altars. Some even brought rats and stray cats. One child brought a caged dove, bobbing and cooing in its innocence. The stench of death and animal terror reached the nostrils of the gods, who resided far beyond high rafters of cedar where aromatic smoke curled, seeking escape. Finely chiselled columns rose loftily, oblivious to the insignificant concerns of jostling festivalgoers.

The people of Actium knew full-scale war was imminent, not least from the numbers of off-duty soldiers that swelled their ranks. They therefore sought assurance from great Apollo that such deprivation and rape of their homesteads would pass them by — if it please Apollo and any other gods present to witness their plight.

Panther clutched Zara's hand and led her closer to the place where priests accepted the alms and sacrifices of an impoverished populace. Her face was shadowed beneath a hooded cape, incongruous in the summer heat but nonetheless essential lest any inquisitive officer should recognise a suspected insurgent. Blood and fear assaulted her senses.

'There.'

Panther pointed to a knot of onlookers crowding around a fanatical priest waving a bloodied ceremonial knife, wild eyes searching for another victim. His simple robes were splattered with blood and grime, and ghostly face-paint made him all the more terrifying. Yet the crowds were drawn to him. He was yelling what might have been messages from the gods in an unknown tongue, a madness that in any other setting would have ostracised him, but he was Apollo's own and the people loved it. Zara watched as the crazed priest leapt onto the stone altar, bare feet slipping on bloody animal innards, just keeping his balance. He continued his tirade, now in common Greek but nonetheless nonsensical.

And Zara recognised him, despite the ghastly disguise.

'He was with Eurycles?' As she said his name, she involuntarily touched the viper brooch that she had been given months ago, back in Samos.

Panther nodded, looking around. Perhaps there were more undercover spies here — but for whom? It didn't matter to Panther, who knew where his loyalties lay. Zara was all that mattered to him. His gaze settled on a young boy at the edge of the crowd. A pair of rustic crutches just about held him upright. One leg was twisted at an unnatural angle, a threadbare tunic barely covered his skinny torso, and his matted hair screamed poverty and pain. As Panther watched him shuffle uncomfortably, the boy turned towards him and winked.

'Ratboy?' Panther mouthed.

Zara had seen him too, though she did not recognise him. She wanted to give him alms, but before she could move the wild priest stole the moment with a startling, drawn-out cry followed by a proclamation.

'The god is here!' he cried. 'He comes with fire and vengeance!'

The crowd gasped, many cowering, others looking skyward as if expecting a flaming chariot to swoop down upon them.

Zara watched him, open-mouthed. Panther chuckled, drawing angry looks from those nearest.

Nothing was going to stop Shoeless the fake priest from enjoying his moment in the limelight. He gave the crowd a madman's glare and cried, 'He comes to rain fire upon those who offend him.' Even the musicians stopped to listen. 'I see flames dripping into a lake of fire as men cry out to be saved. The cowardly, the faithless, the detestable, murderers, the perverted and all liars — they will be thrown into the lake that burns with fire and sulphur. Those who defile his holy precincts will die by the fiery sword.'

A woman wailed and others took up the lament. Zara wondered what she was doing in this cauldron of religious zeal. Even Panther curbed his amusement and other priests nearby stared in amazement.

Shoeless paused, remembering why he was here. He was meant to ingratiate himself with the temple servants, not stir up religious fervour. Palms down, he moved his hands slowly outward, which had a calming effect on his audience. He turned his head sideways, looking up, as if listening to great Apollo himself.

'But wait,' he said, more quietly now. 'He speaks to me.'

This was a great risk. People, even priests, had been stoned for such irreverence. But some in the crowd turned to look at their neighbour with wonderment. They were believers, and now they were hearing this wild man tell them that the god loved the innocent. Romans who came in anger from east and west would suffer and die while innocent Greeks would live in peace and prosperity. Some, clearly off-duty soldiers, growled their complaints, but most were local Greeks who warmed to the message from the god.

The crazed prophet smiled for the first time, paternal and compassionate. Many took an involuntary step closer.

'I am here to tell you that all you innocent lambs will be saved, and now he wishes to show his love for those who dwell in peace.'

A woman shouted, 'Give us a sign!'

'A sign? Do you test the god?'

There was a murmur. Was this allowed? The people were uncertain, but the same woman shouted again with considerable courage, 'Yes!'

'Very well.' Shoeless Luka took a deep breath, puffed out his chest and scanned the crowd. His eyes alighted on a boy leaning on his crutches at the edge of the large gathering.

'Boy, come here...'

Zara and Panther watched in silent amazement even though both knew what was coming, what Shoeless had planned all along. Ratboy played the part superbly. He dragged a foot behind him as he painfully staggered on his supports, grimacing as he came. Shoeless leapt down from the altar. The other priests looked on, partly in disgust, partly intrigued. Who was this deranged newcomer?

Shoeless made no move towards the boy. He stood with welcoming arms outstretched as Ratboy approached. It took an age, but no one spoke. At last the poor boy stood before the priest, head bowed. Ratboy even appeared to be weeping. Never before had the people of Actium seen anything like this. What would this fearsome priest do to the poor child, especially since he still held high a knife dripping with sacrificial blood? There had been no human sacrifice in Actium for many years, although that could not be said for the barbarians on the neighbouring island of Leukas.

Shoeless played to his audience. He held the knife higher, arms still outstretched. He looked across the crowd, then upwards, dark eyes wide in false wonder as if he could see the glorious and terrible gods themselves. This evoked a low murmuring, which swelled like distant thunder as if the deity itself was possessing not only the deranged priest, but also every onlooker. Even Zara was awed and clutched at Panther's arm. Only the other priests moved, taking cautious steps towards this alarming scene where a stranger was taking centre stage in their own domain.

Shoeless turned his gaze on Ratboy. 'My child, come. The god would embrace you.'

If Ratboy and Shoeless had rehearsed this moment, it didn't come off. Ratboy had never submitted to close physical contact with any of *Hera*'s crew and scowled, then took a step back. For a brief moment, Shoeless forgot himself and scowled back, then whispered something with a venom that was not picked up even by those closest. Then he smiled at the crowds, reached out and clasped Ratboy to his bloodstained bosom.

'Demons of Hades, begone!'

He shook the boy so hard that the crutches fell away and Ratboy staggered back, his once useless leg now firm as he fought to keep his balance. He took a few steps and by a greater miracle remembered the part he was to play. He danced. The crowd gasped. Some cheered, some wept, others applauded. Then they surged as one upon the miracle-bringer and mobbed Shoeless, who to his shame forgot all modesty and revelled in their praise. Some forced money on him, which he gladly received, while most begged him to cure various ailments.

The temple's real priests were furious but were too slow against the pressing crowds and couldn't get near Actium's new hero. The city had never seen anything like it, not since a hermit had shown them herbs to cure the barren. Ratboy was forgotten in the crush and stood apart, satisfied with his performance but also confused as to why no one was interested in the recipient of Apollo's grace, only the giver — the channeller of divine power. Bloody Shoeless Luka!

But Zara didn't ignore him and neither did Panther. They couldn't get to Shoeless because of the crush around him, so they went straight to where Ratboy stood. Panther reached him first and slapped him on the back.

'Great performance,' he said, beaming.

Ratboy was amazed to see Panther so far from Samos but was relieved to find someone not much older than himself. And then he saw Zara. He was in awe of this woman and had been briefed to find her if at all possible, and now she stood before him.

'Lady,' he said, bowing, 'we were sent to find you and now you have found us.'

Zara smiled warmly. 'I know they call you Rat or something, but I will not call you that after witnessing such a performance. What shall I call you?'

Ratboy shrugged. 'It's my name. Ratboy. I like it.'

'Hmmm … whatever you say … but we must talk to your friend.'

Shoeless was still being mobbed by the hopeful, and the priests were also trying to reach him. Standing apart and showing no enthusiasm for the crowd's euphoria was a group of three stern-faced men, obviously off-duty soldiers, possibly officers. They were watching Shoeless. Panther, always the sharpest of observers, was watching them.

He tugged Zara's cloak to get her attention. 'Not here,' he said, pointing to the three men. 'We cannot risk you being seen here; word might get back to Publicola.'

Zara was thoughtful. She trusted Panther, who had proved his devotion to her time and again. Reluctant to play on the emotions of one so young, she nonetheless appreciated that he had probably saved her life on more than one occasion.

'You and I will return to our safe place,' she told him. 'But perhaps you and this very clever Rat person can arrange something?'

Ratboy visibly swelled. He saw himself as Panther's equal in the dangerous game of spycraft. And now, without saying anything, his eyes gleamed with pride and he was silently pledged to Zara's service, not least because he knew in his heart that she would become Eurycles' woman. The mother he'd never had.

Shoeless was still being mobbed. The poor and the sick had found new hope and no matter how jealous the temple's priests, the people would no doubt ensure that he was accepted. In the midst of waving arms and hysterical cries of supplication, they could see glimpses of Apollo incarnate. Shoeless may have been overplaying his hand, but he was thoroughly enjoying this new identity.

He probably even believed it.

CHAPTER THIRTEEN

When Lucius Gellius Publicola looked at you with those cold eyes, you had no idea whether you were about to be rewarded or nailed to a crucifixion stake. Most officers were not prepared to take that gamble and avoided him at all costs. Yet the three men who stood before him now considered themselves to be equally as hard as Publicola and stood spear-straight, showing no sign of nerves, confident in the information they had to offer Mark Antony's senior legate. They were members of Publicola's personal *speculatores*, shadowy informers rarely seen in uniform who infiltrated every part of Antony's vast military community, especially non-Roman allies.

Publicola's quarters were sparse yet functional. He sat behind a heavy oak desk appropriate for his rank. A map of the Ambracian gulf covered most of it, leaving enough room for a jug of wine and one goblet. Only Mark Antony himself would ever be offered refreshment, so the three men knew to expect nothing.

Publicola glared at the men. 'So you are telling me the gods are real and the peasants are getting all excited?'

The three remained expressionless, eyes focused somewhere beyond Publicola's shoulder.

'Sir, we are merely reporting our suspicions,' said their leader, Lupus. 'What happened was not natural —'

Publicola slammed his fist on the map, causing the goblet to jump. 'I'm not interested in sorcery and mass hysteria! I don't give a damn about these people and their futile beliefs. Now, tell me the real reason why you are here.'

Lupus hesitated. He was short on evidence, not least because the Egyptian camp had been locked down to all but Mark Antony himself. Mere suspicions didn't hold water for a blinkered disciplinarian like Publicola.

'Spit it out, man, or stop wasting my time.'

Lupus risked looking Publicola in the eye. 'You asked us to watch for a woman in the Egyptian court.'

At last, just the briefest flicker crossed the legate's otherwise impassive face. 'I did. Go on.'

'We think she was there. She was disguised, but we recognised the youth who often visits her. They were together at the temple.'

Another emotion crossed Publicola's face. He frowned. He knew this elusive youth was trouble but had dismissed him as irrelevant — until he had popped up here at Actium and had been seen hovering around the Egyptian queen's encampment.

'And…?'

'They spoke to the lame boy, who turned out not to be lame after all.'

'Perhaps they were just intrigued?'

Lupus returned his gaze to a point behind Publicola. 'Sir, we think they knew this boy. It seemed they were over-friendly.'

'So, a plant. A spy. And the priest?'

'We didn't see them talk to the priest, but he was being mobbed by the peasants. If you want our opinion —'

'That's what you're here for,' Publicola snapped.

'Well, Sir, no one has ever heard of this priest before, so perhaps he has been sent here to ingratiate himself with the temple servants, then…'

'Then send back messages to the enemy about our positions and our navy — is that what you're saying?'

Lupus bit his lip. It seemed so improbable, especially now that he had voiced his suspicions in front of his superior. He said nothing. There was a long silence as Publicola rapped fingers on the desk while continuing his impassive stare. At last, he spoke.

'What of this writer fellow — the woman's brother, I believe?'

'Strabo?' Lupus was pleased to be able to provide a factual answer, for what it was worth. 'He's been gone for days. Word is he is mapping the area.'

'Spying, more like. He was Octavian's man in Rome, was he not? Why is he still breathing?'

There were ways of reminding a superior officer of his precise orders without accusing him of failure, but Lupus couldn't think of them. 'You asked us to watch him, not kill him.'

'So why aren't you watching him?'

Lupus had that sinking feeling, the moment where stomach and bowels churn so much you cannot engage brain and tongue sufficiently to swerve away from guilt or change the subject. But he didn't need to extricate himself, because a messenger arrived and stood panting at the entrance. Publicola gave the new arrival his most fearsome glare and beckoned. The three men gave the messenger space, taking the opportunity to move a few steps back, slightly further from the firing line.

The messenger bowed deeply and handed over a leather case, worn and tattered from continual use since the Parthian campaign. Publicola recognised Mark Antony's seal, broke it and extracted the message with a flourish. He read it slowly, his expression giving nothing away. He dismissed the messenger, briefly studied his map, then turned to Lupus and his two henchmen.

'Watch them all. Find out if this miracle-working priest is a spy and if he is, who sent him. Recruit more men if you need to. Find this Strabo fellow. And bring me enough solid facts to have our hard-working carpenters making a neat row of crucifixion stakes.'

The men saluted and turned to leave, but Publicola called them back.

'And make it quick,' he said. 'This war will be over in a matter of days.'

The fishing boats came in at dawn, fighting for beach space nearest the ox-drawn carts that would take their catch along the winding track to Mark Antony's hungry legions. It had been a good night for the fleet; they had struck lucky when a large shoal of silver tunny had corralled a thousand smaller bluefish close inshore. Bilges heaved with lithe creatures, many yet thrashing in their death throes.

None of the local crews objected to the newcomer, not when the catch was so plentiful and the price higher than any could remember. These foreigners from the south had proved generous and entertaining, always willing to part with coin in the old shack that almost passed for the local tavern. Sour ale tasted better when strangers opened their purses. They could sing, too, and tell tales of heroes of old.

Eurycles felt the keel grind on shingle when the skiff was yet a full spear length from the shore. Without waiting for orders, Niko led the way, leaping into thigh-deep water, followed by Eurycles and two others who heaved on the bow to drag the now-lightened boat to the shore. A dozen villagers, mostly children, were already passing baskets of fish along a chain towards the carts, where an officer was recording the catch. The rewards would be shared equally among each boat-owner.

Those rewards were of little consequence to Eurycles. He scanned the shore's treeline where women waited for their menfolk and was pleased to see Ratboy among them, leaning against a cypress. Niko and the others were hurling the larger fish to shore for collection, but why wasn't Ratboy rushing to assist them? Eurycles was about to call him over when the boy gave a slight shake of his head and with the subtlest movement gestured to his right. Eurycles studied the villagers, all excited at the night's success and chattering animatedly. Except one. This man was dour, dressed to merge inconspicuously whether in a crowd or under woodland cover. But even from this distance, his expression was not inconspicuous; his eyes darted from boat to boat, then towards Ratboy, who was now doing his best to mingle with the crowd.

Eurycles took a gutting knife from his belt, nodded very slowly in Ratboy's direction, then yawned dramatically. His right arm pointed away from the village, the knife indicating the general direction of the communal latrine, a sensible distance from the crude dwellings of fishermen and their families.

Ratboy knew exactly what to do. He had cursed himself for not realising he had been followed until the first silvery light had thrown shadowy movement where there should have been none. But by then, so close to the village, turning back would have been pointless. Whoever was following now knew his destination. But why? Who was this, and was he alone? How much did he know? Were the others in danger? It had been easy enough to mingle with the villagers as they gathered to receive the sea's harvest and identify a lone follower with a soldier's bearing. A man who must die. But how, and where?

Eurycles would know what to do, and the clamour of cowbells and calls to laggards to awake had told him the motley fishing fleet was approaching.

Eurycles did know what to do and Ratboy had understood perfectly. The knife. The latrine. They were thinking as one. Ratboy touched the dagger at his belt and made for the concealed latrine. Eurycles watched him go, then waited as their quarry looked around before following a good distance behind.

Niko, alert as ever, had sensed something was afoot. 'Need me?' he asked quietly, but Eurycles shook his head.

'Finish unloading,' he said without taking his eyes off the shadowy man. 'If I'm not back by then, come and find me. If I'm dead…'

'You'll live,' smiled Niko. 'You've got a bigger mission to accomplish, so this is just practice.'

The old woman squatted over the stinking trench, feet firmly planted on two soiled boards, skirts hitched around her waist. She was oblivious to the smell, which was worse in the summer months because the flushing stream always dried up in the long wait for autumn's rain. She actually preferred this stench to the pervading smell of rotting fish, just by way of a change. But the flies were annoying. Villagers could find the latrine blindfolded just by following the incessant droning of flying insects. She began to hum with satisfaction and allowed herself to linger in the hope of further success — and to give herself a few more moments of peace away from squabbling grandchildren.

She stopped humming when a face peered cautiously around the privacy wall. But she didn't move or speak, just locked eyes with a complete stranger who, crouching low, was studying her intently. She had never seen him before and knew immediately that he was one of those Roman bastards who had come to fight their stupid war on her territory. It wasn't just the short grey hair and the oversized aquiline nose; it was the cold hardness in his eyes. A soldier's eyes. A killer's.

In a slow, deliberate movement, she reached behind her bony rump, fingers finding their target while her angry glare held the Roman's gaze. Then, with unexpected swiftness, she flung excrement which splattered against his shoulder.

The man didn't move. He just stared at her.

The old woman cleaned herself with a handful of hay and stood. She was about to give him a piece of her mind when the Roman's attention was snatched away. He was looking at something beyond her, on the opposite side of the latrine.

'Are you looking for me?'

She turned, almost casually. Nothing surprised her anymore. The newcomer had spoken in Greek, if with a strange accent. She recognised him instantly, the fisherman from the south who had come to their shores a few weeks ago. He was looking straight at the Roman killer and held a gutting knife in his hand.

Still crouching, the Roman stared back but said nothing. Perhaps he didn't speak Greek.

The old woman sighed. 'Look, if you two are going to fight, have the decency to go somewhere else.'

Eurycles laughed. A forced laugh as much to disguise the fear he felt as to distract the Roman's attention, even confuse him. Because at that moment a blade slid across the Roman's throat, leaving a thin red line that suddenly opened grotesquely to belch the man's lifeblood.

The Roman fell forward, his body twitching twice before lying still. Ratboy was left standing with his bloodied knife, shaking with the terror of his first kill. The boy and the merchant-fisherman stood speechless in the stench of filth that now mingled with coppery blood.

Eurycles nodded his admiration.

The woman shrugged and walked away.

Ratboy threw up.

'Drink,' commanded Eurycles. Ratboy simply stared at the cup of ale. His normally bronzed face was the colour of milk, his eyes glazed. Niko ruffled the boy's hair and made encouraging noises. Around them, villagers loudly toasted the success of their night's catch, oblivious to the event that had taken place in their nearby latrine. But Eurycles knew it would only be a matter of time before the body was discovered face down in the overflow pit or the old crone gossiped.

'Drink, then talk to us.' Eurycles' tone was sharper this time.

Ratboy sipped, then deciding the ale tasted better than vomit, drank more deeply. It lightened his mood. If only it had been Mark Antony's throat beneath his blade. He gulped more ale. He was a warrior now — this was what real men did.

'That's enough,' said Eurycles and drank from his own cup. 'Now tell us, who was he?'

Ratboy looked at each of his fellow warriors in turn and thought hard. What had he done since arriving at Actium with Shoeless? Every move had attracted suspicion. He made up his mind not to tell Eurycles the whole story.

'A watcher?'

'You mean a spy?' The *signaculum* identity bronze they had found on the dead man had given no clues — just an eye symbol with no name or number. 'Now tell us who you have spoken to since you went to the temple.'

'Panther.'

'Your friend who helped us at Samos?'

Ratboy nodded. 'And the lady.'

Eurycles leaned forward and failed to keep the spark of enthusiasm from his voice.

'Zara?'

'She has much to tell you.'

'But we must now assume that she or this Panther are being watched. Or both of them. And when the man you killed doesn't return, they will know you are part of a conspiracy, even if they don't know where you are.'

'It's dangerous,' put in Niko. 'But then, war is dangerous.'

Eurycles was thoughtful. His heart was beating faster at the thought of seeing Zara again, but how could this be arranged away from the prying eyes of Mark Antony or, more to the point, that cold-hearted bastard Publicola? He blocked out the hubbub of tavern conversation and tried to think. Where? When?

He was so lost in thought that the tap on his shoulder made him start. He turned and looked into the eyes of the old woman he had last seen walking out of the latrine. Ratboy seemed fearful; Niko was simply amused, but a thousand questions thrashed through his mind. She seemed different to the squatting crone who had been caught up in an unsavoury episode through no fault of her own. She was upright, for a start, and smelled of fresh herbs, not the expected stench of the latrine. Her long grey hair had been combed, and her skirts showed no sign of having been dragged through the latrine's filth.

'Romans are no friends of ours,' she said. Her voice was deep and matriarchal. She looked around and indicated the room's crush of villagers. 'But these are my friends, my children and their children, and you have brought danger to our shore. You must leave.'

Eurycles clasped her bony hand. 'Of course, Grandmother. But where can we go? Where will we find a welcome such as your people have shown us?'

She smiled. 'You are one of us, Eurycles. A Spartan, maybe, but one of us.' She winked mischievously. 'You'll find somewhere to continue your wicked plotting.'

She turned her gaze on Ratboy. 'And as for this boy, he may be an ugly runt, but I like him. He kills Romans.'

CHAPTER FOURTEEN

Mark Antony surveyed the four generals he had summoned to his command pavilion. He had weighted it purposefully in favour of those most likely to back engagement at sea — Publicola, Insteius, Sosius. With his irritable insistence on a land battle as far away from this hellhole as possible, the one dissenting voice, Canidius, would be outnumbered four to one. Antony could even afford to humour him, but not for long. The veteran general would have to be blind not to have seen the preparations undertaken at the sheltered anchorage just a few *stadia* from where they stood.

In the centre of the pavilion was a large table and upon it another clue as plain as the bulbous nose on Canidius's face. It was a work of art. The entire Ambracian basin was mapped in relief, complete with a vibrant blue sea to the west and mountainous terrain to the east. Squares of white-painted wood marked the Antonian camp and legions on the Actium promontory; black squares — and fewer of them — mapped the Octavian camp opposite, across the narrow straits. Three crudely carved ships sat in the Ionian Sea just outside the Ambracian inlet, representing Octavian's fleet of two hundred and fifty warships in three squadrons. These were also painted black. Much larger were the four golden model ships aligned in the inland sea of Ambracia. The implications were clear: Mark Antony's ships were bigger, better and bristling with firepower.

Publius Canidius understood immediately. He shook his head and stabbed a finger at the white camp. 'We have more men and cavalry than that sickly upstart and we should use them.'

Mark Antony smiled. 'My dear Publius, the men are sick and hungry. They need some fresh sea air.' He avoided mentioning the recent defections that had rocked morale of late. The other three remained silent, confident.

'Octavian quakes in his boots at the thought of facing your legions, yet you are thinking of playing into his hands and fighting on his terms.'

If Antony had not been experiencing a rare sober moment, he might have berated his general. But he maintained his smile. 'On the contrary, we will fight on our terms. Tell me, Publius, how these tiny ships —' he pointed to Octavian's fleet, then to his own ships — 'can possibly defeat these magnificent vessels? Can a mosquito penetrate the hide of an elephant?'

Publicola grunted his approval. Insteius and Sosius looked smug. But Canidius wasn't finished.

'Octavian and Agrippa have battled many times at sea, and they know how to win. When have you — we — ever fought in this way?'

'Enough!' Antony's eyes flashed angrily. 'There is no difference. Our ships are floating fortresses. Our artillery will annihilate Octavian's pathetic little ships and our best archers and spearmen will pick off those that come near. And our men won't have to march into battle because our rowers will take them there.'

Now Canidius warmed to his theme and dared to stand up to his superior. He'd done it before and won the argument. 'Our rowers are no better than slaves. They haven't been paid in months, and they are sick and weak. Where is the Egyptian coin they were promised, and where are the provisions that your lascivious queen hoards for her own people? If you don't pay them, they won't row you to victory. If you don't feed them, they couldn't anyway!'

Antony was aghast. He had no sword at his belt, so he bunched his fists instead. 'Get out!' he yelled. 'Go now and send your best cohorts down to the ships immediately.'

Canidius seemed only too happy to obey. He stormed out, muttering as he went. Sosius and Insteius grinned; Publicola said nothing. He was studying the relief map intently. When calm had been restored, he asked quietly, 'How will you deploy the Egyptian ships?'

Mark Antony brought himself under control and took a deep breath. 'Here's the plan,' he said. 'The local soothsayers say this wind will not abate for a few days yet. When it does, and when the seas calm, Sosius, Insteius and I will lead our fleet out and annihilate those little toy ships. We will sail right through them and sink them all.'

Publicola coughed. 'And the ships under my command?'

'They will go in the van, right out there in front — but not you, my dear friend Lucius.' Publicola frowned. He thought he guessed what was coming. 'You, Lucius Gellius Publicola, will hang back alongside the Egyptian fleet. When the time is right, and when Queen Cleopatra Philopator chooses to follow, you will protect her and her ships by sailing out with them, sinking any of the enemy that remain afloat.'

'And then?'

'And then you celebrate and await my orders.'

Somewhat confused by these instructions, Publicola felt the time was right to convey his most recent discoveries. 'Sir,' he ventured, 'have these orders been discussed in the Egyptian camp?'

'Yes. Why do you ask?'

'Because I have reason to believe that Octavian's spies, or at least the rat Agrippa's, have been eavesdropping and they may be close to betraying your intentions.'

Antony smiled again. 'Is that so? Then I can think of no one better than you, dear Lucius, to catch them, torture them, and give them the slowest, most ghastly death your wicked mind can dream up.'

It was Publicola's turn to smile — a rare event for him. He nodded and went to do his worst.

CHAPTER FIFTEEN

Taking a cartload of fish into Mark Antony's sprawling army camp was a slow process, not just because the ox that drew it could not be hurried but also because of the endless checkpoints. They had to pass through the tent-rows of three outlying legions, where guards insisted on lifting the covers before turning away in disgust: the noonday heat and increasing attention from insistent flies did not present an appetising prospect, even among the starving.

Eurycles was uncomfortable. Sweat was running down his neck and a linen scarf around nose and mouth was failing to keep the pervading stench at bay. Beside him, Ratboy simply stared wide-eyed at Roman soldiers about their duties, some sharpening weapons in front of sun-bleached canvas tents, others under marching drill in full armour. Despair hung over Mark Antony's camp like leaden thunderclouds.

'Where?' asked Eurycles. The heat made talking difficult, let alone breathing.

But Ratboy had no idea where the Egyptian camp lay. He scratched his head, thinking.

'Panther will know.'

'So how do we find your friend?'

Ratboy shrugged again. 'He'll find us.'

They continued for some time in silence before Eurycles decided to ask for directions. He pulled hard on the ox rein to bring the lumbering beast to a halt close to a small group of soldiers, one of them wearing a cloak that might set him apart as an officer. He knew the risks — half-starved soldiers might not only steal their cargo of fish, but could also slaughter the ox for the legion's cauldrons. The possible officer turned to study them. A filthy head scarf covered what was probably a bald head, hollow cheeks and sunken eyes expressing weariness and hunger, yet his back was straight and his shoulders were squared, as an officer's should be. Four men with him stared blankly.

'What do you want?' It was not a polite enquiry. It was spoken in crude Greek, probably picked up during months of campaigning in Asia Minor, and Eurycles sensed the arrogant nuances of a Roman addressing local serfs. Not unexpected. He hooked the scarf from his face and forced a smile.

'We have a delivery for the Egyptian camp. Can you direct us?'

The man's fists bunched. He took several steps towards the visitors, pointing at Eurycles. 'Whatever it is you have in that cart, those Egyptians don't deserve it,' he said, his voice conveying pure hatred. 'Unless it's poisoned, and you can kill the queen.'

His venom confirmed what Eurycles already suspected — that Cleopatra had debased Mark Antony and undermined any hope of mounting a true Roman offensive. That ambivalent siren was the true cause of the rampant demoralisation in the ranks of what had once been an unstoppable fighting force.

Eurycles said nothing as the officer, muttering curses, walked to the cart and lifted the cover. He recoiled in disgust, then studied the driver and his boy assistant.

'Are you local?' he asked, eyes narrowed but calmer now. A conversation with a friend that very morning came to mind — something about a network of spies possibly working with those foul Egyptians. It involved a boy about the same age as this fidgeting brat here.

'Good catch last night,' said Eurycles, a thumb over his shoulder, indicating the general direction of the shore. This vague answer was met with a frosty stare and a long silence. Eurycles held the officer's gaze and Ratboy stopped fidgeting.

Eventually the officer said, 'Follow this track out of our camp, skirt to the right around the Sixth and you'll see the fancy Egyptian tents. Security's tight as a locust's arse, though. Take your time and maybe your fish will rot their guts.'

Eurycles tapped the ox's rump with his driver's pole, encouraging the beast with a 'hup hup', and the cart moved off. The sullen officer watched them go.

Then he turned on his heel and went to find his friend Lupus.

Panther spotted them on the track leading to the Egyptian camp. Hood up, he weaved among crowds of soldiers and civilians to shadow the cart that was now in a slow-moving queue of motley wagons and handcarts bearing supplies of questionable quality. The air was thick with dust and arguments. Word had spread that the Egyptians were paying a higher rate than any of Mark Antony's legions, attracting hordes of impatient farmers, fishermen and traders. These in turn brought numerous youths from the surrounding settlements, each offering a shortcut or a back door to foreign gold.

Ratboy felt a tug on his sleeve and turned to see his friend sauntering beside the fish-cart. Panther pointed to a small group of peasants that had gathered nearby. One of them was a priest — a very familiar priest.

'Ignore them for now,' said Panther hurriedly. 'They're being watched. It's not safe.'

Before he averted his gaze, Eurycles noticed that Strabo was there too, in animated conversation with Shoeless Luka. While he was glad his man had made contact, he worried that the Romans and perhaps the Egyptians also had proved cleverer than expected and had rumbled their plan to find out Mark Antony's intentions. He looked around for suspicious-looking characters and decided that this description could fit any number of soldiers, couriers or off-duty men as there were so many milling around the approaches to Queen Cleopatra's camp.

Panther whistled, and one of his gang sauntered to the fish-cart. 'We'll take it from here,' the youth said with quiet confidence, 'and I'll arrange a meeting.'

'Who with?' Eurycles asked.

'Why, the lady Zara, of course,' Panther replied. 'But not until dusk, away from here. Away from prying eyes.'

Eurycles felt a thrill of excitement. He longed to see her again and wished it was in circumstances other than this ghastly atmosphere of war, sickness and deprivation.

Panther's friend leapt to the driver's seat vacated by Eurycles while Ratboy vaulted effortlessly to the ground and melted into the crowds. The cart moved off, immediately aiming to jump the queue with the impetuosity of youth.

'Follow me,' Panther said. Eurycles didn't hesitate. He was going to meet Zara as soon as the sun set and gave them the cover of darkness. He looked up and saw that the sun was already dropping to the western horizon.

His heart beat faster.

A firm breeze whispered through the pines surrounding a clearing midway between the camps of the legions and the temple of Apollo. Eurycles could hear the crashing of waves beneath the cliffs of Actium just five hundred paces distant. He sat on a fallen tree trunk, listening to the gradually diminishing song of a thousand cicadas. It seemed so far from the stench and squalor of the legionary camps.

Panther had told him to wait in the clearing. How he wished it could have been in Taenarum's best tavern or somewhere more exotic, like Sparta or Athens or even Rome. He had never been to Rome, but he had heard the tales of majestically pillared buildings, gloriously dressed women and haughty nobles dressed in extravagant togas. He thought back to his last meeting with Zara and decided he preferred the street fayre of Samos. But she would like Taenarum best. No frills, just good company, simple food and country wine. Laughter and memories, a stroll arm-in-arm back to a clean and comfortable house, and then...

Did she feel the same?

The last of the sunlight was no more than a golden glow on the tops of weaving pine needles above. A night cricket took over from the cicada symphony. He thought he heard a twig crack underfoot and peered into the murky woods. Zara? Or the enemy? His hopes pitched and plunged like his fishing boat in a squall.

It was Zara. She stood at the edge of the clearing, dappled light fighting dusk on her strong features. She was dressed in clothes suited to this wild countryside, with a woollen cloak clasped tight around her midriff. Eurycles couldn't distinguish the colours — perhaps green and brown, a suitable clandestine blend. Strands of dark hair escaped the confines of the cloak's hood.

She smiled.

Eurycles' heart missed a beat. He stood and almost stumbled, cursing his clumsiness. He wished he had made a welcoming fire or brought some delicacies to enjoy while they talked. Too late now. He cursed himself again.

'*Khaire*,' he said, and that simple 'hello' was as hollow as a drum.

'Eurycles,' she said, her voice like liquid gold.

She came to him with languid steps, and he summoned graciousness and invited her to sit on the log. She gathered her cloak across her knees and sat. Was she leaning towards him? No, perhaps just adjusting the folds. He didn't know what to say. It had been too long, and his longings for her had raced ahead of their proper place.

She smiled again, but it was too dark now and might have been his imagination. He felt her warmth, and she smelled faintly of some kind of spice.

'We don't have much time,' she said.

With enormous courage, Eurycles clasped her hand where it lay between them, on the tree trunk. She didn't withdraw. He remembered why he was here. 'What's happening?'

She answered with a question of her own. 'Is Octavian's fleet arrayed?'

Eurycles knew exactly why she was asking this — not to warn her mistress the queen, but to find out where the true fighting might eventually take place.

'They are ready and can form up at very short notice,' he replied. 'But the weather…'

'Isn't right for a sea battle,' she interrupted. 'I know this because I listen. But as soon as the wind calms, that is where Mark Antony will fight.'

Eurycles fought to control his desire. This was why he was here. 'Not on land, then?' he managed.

'His legions are hungry and demoralised, and many defect every day. He would rather fight on the sea.'

'That might be his best option. His ships are huge. Who can fight them?'

Zara laughed. 'Agrippa can, of course.'

He laughed too. 'He's done it before. Mark Antony hasn't.'

Her look was suddenly serious, her eyes exploring his. 'But there's something that Mark Antony doesn't know.'

Eurycles took a moment to collect himself. He was not here for romance; he was here to spy. He instinctively touched his viper brooch. 'Go on.'

'The queen has no intention of fighting.'

'What…?'

'Her only wish is to get away from this dreadful place, and she will lead her fleet straight back to Egypt.'

Eurycles was aghast. Thoughts flashed through his mind as he considered what this information would mean to Agrippa. He moved closer and almost whispered, 'She would betray Mark Antony?'

'The great Mark Antony will follow her, no matter what happens out there.'

'And leave his legions stranded here?'

'Many of them have orders to embark tomorrow. My queen is loading her gold and her own guard onto her ships. They will sail as soon as the storms desist, and they know the winds will be fair for sailing south. They always are at this time of year. But Mark Antony will hurl his ships at Octavian's and hope to destroy them before he escapes.'

'Escapes? He is defeated already, then?'

'Of course. He gave up weeks ago. He thinks he will have a better chance fighting Octavian in Africa or Egypt. He knows now that he has made a huge mistake.'

Eurycles was silent as he took this in. He needed to take this message back to Agrippa as soon as possible. The weather might break, and Agrippa had to be told where the fight would take place.

'And you? Will you come with me?'

'Yes.'

They were leaning towards each other, ever closer. Like lovers caught up in the horror of war, they felt a faint glimmer of hope that something better lay ahead.

'Run!' The untimely interruption was Panther's. He burst into the clearing, Ratboy close behind. 'Run! Publicola's men are here!'

CHAPTER SIXTEEN

They should have run but they didn't.

Eurycles swiftly appraised the problem and tried to remain calm. He could hear an approaching commotion, but it was now too dark to see anything more than a few strides away. Panther was quick to see an alternative to flight.

'We'll create a diversion,' the youth said, panting. 'They'll follow us while you hide.'

'How many men?' Eurycles asked, looking from Panther to Ratboy. Zara was already searching for a suitable hiding place.

'Probably twenty, fanned out and searching,' said Ratboy, and Panther nodded in agreement. 'Strabo and Shoeless are following behind them to see what happens.'

'Good. But before you go, listen to me carefully.' The sound of men crashing through woodland was becoming worryingly close. 'If we are taken, get word to Shoeless and Strabo that Mark Antony will soon bring his ships out to fight, but the Egyptians intend to flee. Have them get word to Myron and thence to Agrippa.'

Ratboy nodded, nervously biting his lip.

Eurycles ruffled his hair. 'Now go.'

Zara tugged at Eurycles' arm. 'Over here,' she said, pulling him towards tangled undergrowth trapped by a fallen tree leaning on its neighbour, branches still thick with pine needles. They began to burrow in the soft vegetation while Panther and Ratboy laid a noisy trail of relentless chatter and broken branches away from the hiding place.

They lay close together as the soldiers approached. Eurycles could feel Zara's breath on his cheek. He was surprised to find their fingers entwined, and he marvelled at the feel of firm muscles where their thighs touched. He leaned his forehead closer to hers. 'Lie still,' she whispered as they sensed the first of the men passing. There was a muffled shout as one of them heard the youths' decoy run. Several surged away from the hiding place with renewed intent.

But it hadn't occurred to them, nor to Panther and Ratboy, that one of the pursuers might have a dog. It wasn't a hunting dog, and the soldier had only brought the mangy creature with him because the two had become inseparable ever since the others in their tent had been dissuaded from eating it. It was a long-legged mongrel with protruding ribs showing through patchy grey fur and a long nose that now poked into their hiding place. The dog whined and scrabbled at the ground, hoping that whoever was in there might have a scrap of food to spare.

The soldier peered in to see what his dog had found, prodding at the foliage with his sword.

Lucius Gellius Publicola did not conduct interrogations under the nose of fellow commanders, and certainly not anywhere near those objectionable Egyptians — especially when one of his captives was so clearly favoured by their queen. Neither did he interrupt his dining arrangements to conduct interrogations in the evening. Let these two miserable spies spend a cold night fearing the dawn and his wrath. His orders had been clear — treat them harshly, but do not touch the woman until he was finished with them. The men understood this of their general, but few of them realised he preferred young males.

So with the dawn he stepped outside his lavish tent, pulled his regal cloak tight to ward off the chill and summoned two of his guards. He then set off on the long walk to the clifftop gaol he had constructed not far from Apollo's Temple. This was his favourite place during the long days of boredom. It was where riffraff could be beaten to death for no other reason than he liked the sight and smell of blood. It was also where the disobedient were punished and cowardly soldiers were executed. He had chosen the vicinity of the temple because he rightly sensed that the locals favoured the occasional human sacrifice. Publicola had plenty of candidates, although simply flinging them off the cliff was barely satisfying, so he preferred to crucify them first. The sight of screaming victims tumbling into the roiling sea below, arms outstretched on the crossbeam, was much more like it. May it please the gods as much as it pleased him. He hummed quietly as he walked, taking deep breaths of air less stale than that of the camp.

Panther woke with a start. He had tried to stay awake while he watched Publicola's gaol throughout the night, but sleep had overcome him at last. He saw the general and two guards approaching and breathed a sigh of relief that Ratboy, Strabo or Shoeless weren't being dragged to the torture chambers, which meant they must have escaped to alert their friends. He had told Ratboy everything he knew about the ghastly practices that went on at the clifftop and begged him to send word to the Egyptian camp before fleeing to find Myron, although he doubted they would listen to the strange child. He looked across to the row of stakes on the cliff edge, stark against the grey dawn like titans' teeth, and shuddered.

They had been kept apart through the night. Eurycles had been chained with his arms above his head, looped over a beam. The cell was dark and stank of faeces and urine, and by what little light filtered through a high opening and gaps in a shoddily built roof, he could see that prisoners were not given the luxury of a latrine or an outside wall to piss on. He could barely see through his left eye, which had borne the full brunt of a soldier's fist to silence him, and his groin and back ached from the kicking he had received when he had fallen.

He dared to hope that Zara had not been maltreated. These men had been starved of the company of women, and he had spent the long hours dreaming of what he would do to any that touched her. He had called her name several times and strained to listen for disturbances but had heard nothing apart from indecipherable groans of other prisoners. None of them were female. Perhaps she was too far away or had been taken to the Roman camp.

A key turned in the door's lock. Publicola entered. Behind him was a brutish-looking gaoler carrying several ugly implements at his belt. Publicola smiled, then held a cloth to his nose as his glance took in the damp stains on the front of Eurycles' breeches.

'Name?'

Eurycles just stared at him. The backhand across his face stung and he felt a trickle of blood.

'When I ask you a question, you answer immediately. Every time you fail to provide an answer, I will send another man to satisfy himself with your woman. Understand?'

'Yes.' The backhand brought more blood, Publicola's rings opening a gash on his cheek.

'You address me as "Sir". Understand?'

'Yes, Sir.'

'Name?'

'Eurycles, Sir.'

'That's better. We're going to get along just fine.' Publicola narrowed his eyes, studying the bruised and bleeding face. 'Have we met before?'

Eurycles hesitated. It was a difficult question. Perhaps a trick question? Would this Roman remember the *principia* at Samos? He hesitated too long, and this time the backhand was to his other cheek.

'Have we met before?'

'Yes, Sir.'

'The right answer. Now, tell me why you were in Samos.'

'To deliver letters, Sir.'

'Who to?'

'I gave them to you, Sir.'

'And who else?'

'I can't remember, Sir.'

Publicola studied him. 'Try this. Titius and his uncle Plancus. Correct?'

'I can't remember, Sir.'

Publicola turned to the soldier behind him. 'Take a finger and give it to the dog that found them.'

The gaoler took rusty pincers from his belt, reached up and severed the little finger from Eurycles' left hand. There was just a brief moment before the pain kicked in then Eurycles screamed. The finger landed on the floor. The soldier picked it up and leaned outside the cell door. 'Macko! For your dog.' He threw the finger into the corridor. Eurycles felt a wave of nausea and tried to stop himself sobbing.

'Try again,' said Publicola, 'or the next finger will belong to the woman.'

'Yes…' The agony made it hard to speak. 'Yes, I was given letters for these men, but Zara had nothing to do with it … Sir.'

'So tell me, who gave you these letters?'

Eurycles knew it was all over for him, but he might be able to save Zara. 'Marcus Agrippa, Sir.'

'You realise you are confessing to being our enemy?'

Eurycles nodded. His gorge rose and he knew he was going to throw up. 'But Zara knew nothing of this,' he managed. 'She was just someone I met while I was there, and I came here to find her.'

'How sweet. Young love. Poems will be written and songs sung.' Publicola turned to the gaoler and winked. The gaoler laughed. 'So now I am going to talk to the young lady and see if your stories tally.'

He turned to leave, then looked back, his hand reaching into his pocket. 'So tell me, you filthy Greek spy, what is this?' He held up a viper brooch, whether his or Zara's, Eurycles couldn't tell.

It seemed like hours but was probably less than one when Publicola returned. The sound of Roman boots on the stone floor outside his cell sounded to him like an executioner's drum. Eurycles had passed in and out of consciousness, and now the dim light was enough to hurt his eyes. His head throbbed and he realised he had soiled himself.

'Let him down,' Publicola said to the gaoler. 'We're done here.'

The gaoler unlocked the chains and Eurycles collapsed onto the floor. Publicola squatted next to him.

'I understand,' he said, stroking the Greek's shoulder. 'You've been caught up in a mess not of your own making. All you were doing was trying to make an honest living and deliver messages to Titius and Plancus. You did that — well done.'

Eurycles looked up into Publicola's eyes and saw nothing but coldness.

'But the trouble is,' continued the Roman general, 'you couldn't leave it there, could you?' His hand reached to Eurycles' bloodied cheek, patting sympathetically. 'You recruited an innocent woman who was serving our cause, and you pumped her for information.' He chuckled. 'You probably just pumped her.'

Eurycles' mind raced. What had Zara said? He trusted her and decided that Publicola was bluffing.

'Please let her go, Sir. She is innocent. I have been foolish, but she has always been loyal to Queen Cleopatra and Mark Antony. I don't know anything. But kill me and let her go.'

Publicola scratched his chin. 'Hmmm. I am sure you're right.' He patted the bloody cheek again. 'You'll have to die of course, but what shall we do with the lady?' He turned to the gaoler, who bared his teeth in an evil grin.

'I think the gods are tiring of us all. What we need is a sacrifice.'

CHAPTER SEVENTEEN

Too weak to move, Eurycles lay on the floor of his cell for what seemed like hours, sharp pain throbbing along his arm where it met the duller ache of his head and shoulders, leaving him barely conscious. He tried to force himself to move, if only to tear some clothing to wrap the mangled mess of his left hand. The cell became unbearably hot as the sun climbed. Sweat mingled with blood and soon the flies came, feasting on faeces and the wounds on his hand and face.

No one came in. The only relief was that the questions had stopped. Eurycles knew there were soldiers nearby because he could hear barked orders and the sounds of hammering. He thought he heard chanting in the distance but dismissed it as delirium. He thought about praying, not for himself but for Zara, but in his confusion he couldn't think which god might be able to help her. He rebuked himself for self-pity and from somewhere summoned enough strength to crawl to the cell door in the hope that it hadn't been locked. It had. He sat with his back to the door and looked around for anything he might use as a weapon. Nothing. Not even the chains that had held him while the bastard Publicola had assaulted him. He had one functioning hand and was weak from blood loss. There was little hope of fighting his way out.

He must have passed out again. He slowly became aware of a key turning in the lock and the heavy door pushing against his back. There was a shout of 'Move, slug!' Then a firmer thrust left him sprawling in stinking urine. Rough hands lifted him — there were two brutes — and he swung his good arm at the nearest. He was too weak, and the gaoler laughed cruelly. His hands were roped behind him, ending any slim hope that he would be set free. The gaolers worked in silence. He wanted to ask them what was going to happen, but his head throbbed so badly that he all he could do was groan. They pushed him roughly along a corridor and into the prison's courtyard, where bright sunlight assaulted his senses. The main gates were open, facing the cliff edge. Beyond the opening, he could make out a large crowd, and now he realised he hadn't imagined the chanting. His vision was hazy but there were a lot of people, and they weren't all soldiers. He thought it must be a religious gathering; this was confirmed when he made out a line of old men in priestly garb.

The crowd hushed and parted when his gaolers pushed him forward. They seemed awed, perhaps sympathetic towards this dishevelled creature wearing a soiled and bloodied tunic with no shoes, his face bruised and blood-crusted. The flies followed him, trying to resume their gruesome feast. He staggered and looked around for Zara. She was nowhere to be seen, so he looked at the faces that stared back, hoping to see a friend at least, even though he had sent them all away to carry word of… He tried to remember what he had asked them to do, but his mind was a fog of confusion.

'Move.'

One of the jailers prodded him with his sword. He felt the point pierce his skin, but he didn't care anymore. The chanting started again, and he realised it came from the line of priests. The crowd parted further, a hundred pairs of eyes watching in silence. The only sounds were the buzz of flies and the ocean somewhere below.

At last he saw Zara.

There was a platform built on the edge of the cliff. Before it stood a dozen Roman guards in full armour. Behind them were steps leading up to a stage built with crude scaffolding, which appeared to be cantilevered to extend over the cliff edge. Above it was a wooden contraption that supported a beam, to which ropes and pulleys were attached. Standing in the middle was Publicola, dressed in a white priestly toga and carrying an olive branch. Beside him, guarded by a masked gaoler, was Zara. She was also dressed in pure white and appeared to be unharmed. She stood defiantly upright, her hands tied loosely before her, her hair blowing in the wind.

Eurycles cried out and stumbled a few paces toward her before being hauled back. The crowd moved further away from the unfortunate, assuming him to be a criminal or somehow unclean. His soiled and bloody appearance was in stark contrast to the apparent virgin on the sacrificial stage.

Zara saw him. They locked eyes — hers startled and horrified, his full of despair and anger. He struggled to free himself from the grip of his two guards, but she subtly shook her head. In that moment he knew she was resigned to her fate, and he should not draw attention to himself. But he knew he was going to die, and now he was desperate to save her. He began to shout, 'She is innocent!' Before he could finish, the pommel of a gladius crashed into the back of his skull. He collapsed to his knees. A gaoler's boot between his shoulders kicked him to the ground before rough hands grabbed him under the armpits and dragged him to Publicola's dais, leaving him prostrate before the row of guards.

'People of Actium!' Publicola's powerful voice rang out. 'Today your fortunes will change.' He paused for effect, making a sweeping gesture to encompass all the silent faces before him. 'It is not your fault that famine and pestilence has befallen you. You are innocent bystanders and have the misfortune to be caught up in the designs of evil people.' He paused again, and half turned to glare at Zara. The crowd murmured. They did not know who she was, nor did they fully understand who this Roman priest represented. For all they knew, he might be Mark Antony himself.

'I have heard it said that Apollo has already shown you his kindness, and now we stand on sacred ground to ask the god to restore your fortunes.' At this the murmurs grew, and many nodded their agreement. 'But how can we ask this of Great Apollo when we have done nothing to atone for our sin? And what is that sin?' The crowd now hung on his words expectantly, hoping the sin was not theirs.

'The Great Sin against the god is this — that we allowed a foreign power into our land.' At this, the crowd edged towards anger. 'Not just foreigners, but heretics. Heretics!' Now some shouted their approval, and the people of Actium gave voice to their hostility.

Eurycles, who had crawled to his knees, summoned the strength to shout, 'What has this to do with us?' but his objection was drowned out by the surging crowd.

Publicola held up his hands to bring calm. When he spoke again, his voice dripped with reason. 'Whose land is this? It is yours, of course. You are Greeks, and you must not give it up.'

The lone voice of an old man interjected, 'So what are you Romans doing here?'

Under different circumstances, the man's life might have ended abruptly, but Publicola simply smiled at him. He knew his argument could now easily expose his hypocrisy. So he returned to his theme.

'The Egyptians have brought their false gods to your lands and angered *our* gods. That is why we must appease Great Apollo, right here, right now, so that we can return to peace and prosperity.' He turned again to Zara and raised a trembling finger. 'According to your rites, a virgin must be sacrificed. Here is that Egyptian virgin.'

'No!' shouted Eurycles, but no one heard him in the clamour of cheers and applause. A gaoler's boot pushed him to the ground once more.

Publicola nodded to the masked man standing beside Zara, and he in turn called three men to assist him. One hauled on one of the ropes and a large wooden cross was raised a few feet from where it lay on the platform. The other two grabbed Zara and before she could put up a fight had loosed her bonds, thrown her roughly onto the cross and lashed her hands to the crossbeam and her feet to the upright. As she protested, a cloth was thrust into her mouth. Eurycles struggled to rise but was pinned to the ground by a Roman boot.

Now Publicola addressed a further problem that the more intelligent people present might raise. 'But Egypt isn't the only problem here,' he said. This recaptured the crowd's attention. 'No, indeed, there is another evil force at play. Since all of Greece was given to Mark Antony to rule in benevolence and kindness, another force has entered the picture. Rome! The pretender Octavian, who dares to call himself Caesar, is here —' he waved across the straits to the northern shore, where everyone knew the legions of Rome were encamped and their ships rode at anchor — 'and he will rape your women and sow salt in your fields. He has sent his spies to turn you against your peaceful rulers, and now we must show Apollo that we will not tolerate such indignity and trespass.'

The crowd cheered. Some even dared to think that Apollo would drive out all Romans as well as Egyptians and were ready to cling to whatever hope this strange priest offered them.

'Where are these spies?' shouted the same old man. 'Crucify them.'

'We have one of them right here among you,' smiled Publicola. 'We found him conspiring with Egypt!' Some gasped, but Publicola wasn't finished. Throwing his head back for effect as the priest of Apollo, he pointed at Eurycles and proclaimed, 'Here is the spy!' He then pointed at the forlorn figure of Zara. 'And he conspired with Egypt through her!'

The crowd knew it: the perfect sacrifice. No one questioned whether she was a virgin as ritual demanded or had in fact been seduced by the Roman spy. None even knew that the suspect was not even a Roman. But they wanted to appease the god and now they had been shown the way. They clamoured for both to be sacrificed in the traditional manner by hurling them over the cliff, albeit with the added spice of crucifixion.

But Publicola had one more trick to win the crowd. He nodded to his executioner again. The three men went about their swift work, heaving Eurycles to the platform while the cross was flipped. They then lashed the bruised, wounded and battered Spartan back-to-back with Zara. They tried to speak to each other, but the crowd noise rose to fever pitch. They knew what was coming.

Publicola grinned. He was happy with his oratory, a real crowd-pleaser. He had to raise his voice for even the nearest to hear his conclusion.

'The god will choose. One will die, one may live. Or more likely, both will die.' As he spoke, a flock of birds flew south, so close to the cliff top that those nearest could hear the rush of beating wings. Publicola pointed regally to the departing flock. 'See, the god has spoken. He accepts your sacrifice!'

He nodded to his men, who heaved on the ropes to pull the cross upright. Both Eurycles and Zara were lashed tight and unable to move.

But Publicola hesitated. From the corner of his eye, he saw a squadron of men marching towards the sacrificial site and knew they were not his men or Mark Antony's. They wore the colours and armour of Egyptians. He must hurry. He ordered the guards to form up and block the path of the approaching Egyptians, then turned to study his victims.

The sheer terror in their eyes gave him intense pleasure. The base of the cross dragged on the platform, the groaning support ropes tied tightly to a stanchion. It leaned over the chasm. The masked executioner held a sword over the ropes and watched his commander-priest.

Publicola gave the signal.

The sword fell, the polished blade flashing bright as it severed the ropes in one powerful blow. The crowd gasped as the heavy wooden cross toppled slowly, then disappeared over the precipice with its sacrificial victims. Soldiers and peasants alike stared in silence at the spot where the atoning gift to Apollo was no more. As they gaped, a strange thing happened. A lithe youth, stripped to the waist and holding a curved dagger, sprinted past the distracted guards and onto the dais, slashing ineffectually at a surprised Publicola as he passed like a skimming *ballista* bolt. He leapt into the void, arms and legs wheeling frantically before disappearing from view.

It was not a choice that Panther had made with any reason or deliberation. He would follow the woman he adored and had sworn to protect. He had failed in the latter cause. He would follow her now, even if death was inevitable.

He was not afraid.

PART THREE: FIREFIGHT

CHAPTER EIGHTEEN

Coastal Seas off Actium, Greece, the last day of Sextilis (August), 31BC

Eurycles retched and choked on bitter bile, a strange whistling noise assaulting his senses. Fleetingly, he saw clouds before being swamped once again by the frothy swell. He tried not to breathe in the salty flood, but he had no control over his body, his mind promising peace at last after the tumbling, chaotic drop, the final few heartbeats. Could he hear the cries of gulls, or was it his own scream? Or Zara's?

Zara. He tried to call to her but choked again. He fought his bonds but couldn't move. In fact, he couldn't feel his legs and arms, and he cursed their disobedience. His head lolled, the only part of him that moved, and again he saw sky and clouds — which meant that Zara couldn't. At last he found his voice and tried to call again, but he knew it was no more than a weak groan. He cursed the gods for choosing life for him and decided he would defy them all and die with her, right here, right now. A wave crashed over him, rocking the cross to which he was bound, and he opened his mouth to welcome death. He would be with her in the underworld.

But it was not bitter seawater that filled his lungs. He gulped damp air. Beautiful, fresh air, the very breath of Apollo. He marvelled at its sweetness and breathed again. The underworld, perhaps. He realised that he could see around him, not just sky and clouds but rolling waves and a murky horizon. Then he noticed a sea creature at his feet advancing cautiously toward him, its weight tipping the base of the cross slowly into the depths and his head clear of the water. He looked again and saw that the creature was human and held a knife between its teeth, its dripping hair framing intense, wild eyes.

Panther.

Eurycles dared to hope. He twisted his head and thought he could see Zara's dark hair trailing like weed, swirling in the swell rebounding from the cliff face. His senses began to return — the awful sensation of falling, the rush of air, the sudden plunge into darkness. He could now see the height of the cliff, at least five times a ship's mast. Surely no one could survive that — but he had. He peered again and saw Zara's head emerge from the angry water, hair now hanging limp, concealing her face. He realised he could feel movement on his legs and his first selfish thought was that he wasn't dead. Panther's scrabbling had caused no pain, so perhaps he had no broken bones.

Panther was now attempting to heave the cross further out of the water by leaning back, but it was a dead weight for one so slight. Eurycles could see he was weeping, close to panic. He forced himself to cry out, 'Cut my bonds so I can help!' He wasn't sure if Panther heard him above the enveloping crash of surf around the cliff base, but the boy knew what to do.

Panther dragged himself closer to Eurycles, hooked an arm around his neck and with his other hand took the blade from between his teeth. He reached to his right and began to saw at the bonds that held both Eurycles' and Zara's arms on the crossbeam. A wave surged over the struggling boy, but he didn't falter in his mission. A strand frayed and then broke free, but there were several turns of the thick rope. He cut the next and the ropes loosened.

Shivering with shock and cold, Eurycles pulled an arm free and knew that if she was still alive, Zara could do the same. He twisted his body, gasping as pain surged through his mutilated hand, but now he had one arm to fight for Zara's life. He reached over his right shoulder where Panther was already grasping for her, trying to pull her face free from the foaming sea, and clutched a handful of her hair. His arm, his whole body was shaking uncontrollably, but he drew strength from Panther's dogged determination and together they heaved her head free of the waves. Now he could see her face. A peaceful face, as if she slept. 'Breathe, please breathe,' he gasped. But she didn't.

'Hold her,' cried Panther, who set about cutting free the remaining crossbeam rope. Now their upper bodies were free, but the weight of the cross was forcing Zara's head beneath the surface. Panther handed the knife to Eurycles, who knew what each of them must do. He didn't wait to assist the youth in twisting Zara under the crossbeam so he could hold her above the waves; instead he reached down to the bonds at their feet. This resulted in the cross lifting clear again, and while he cut as firmly as his shaking arms would allow, he prayed that Panther was as strong a swimmer as the youths of Taenarum.

Suddenly their feet were free. Both of them were free. Panther hooked an arm beneath Zara's shoulder, her face barely above the water, and began to pull strongly towards the cliff base, where more danger lay. Eurycles swiftly studied the rocky shore where seething seas hammered at the immobile cliff face. The rocks were like jagged teeth, except one which was flat and covered with dark weed. It was not too far away, yet seemed so far in this convulsion of elements. He took a bearing on the rock, let go of the cross and swam after Panther and Zara.

It seemed to take an age, and the sea fought to keep its victims as first Panther then Eurycles clambered onto the chosen platform. Even the rock itself seemed to fight them, delivering bruises and scratches. Weed clawed at Zara as they dragged her limp body out of the sea's desperate clutches. Panther was pleading with her to wake, shaking her shoulders, weeping as he cried, 'Don't die, lady, *don't die*!' But Eurycles the sailor knew what to do. He had saved crew young and old from Poseidon's clutches. He thrust the panicking youth aside, grasped Zara's body beneath the shoulders and manoeuvred her to the rock's edge. Ignoring the pain of salt in reopened wounds, he flipped her body so that her head and neck faced down into the depths, straddled her back and began to press down firmly and rhythmically. It was a simple problem he must solve if Zara was to come back from the dead. Just as a boat cannot sail when the sea is inside it, this woman could not breathe when the water was inside her. He was patient, his hands pushing up from her lower back, but his mind was racing, pleading to the gods to let her return to him. A sudden gush of clear water from her mouth gave him hope and she coughed. He pushed again and as more came he felt her stirring, just a sudden spasm of the muscles in her back. She coughed again and gulped in air. With Panther's gentle help, Eurycles pulled her fully onto the rock, then helped her to sit upright. She opened her eyes and vomited green bile. Eurycles had never loved anyone more than in that moment. Panther hugged her; it was the first time he had dared to touch this noble woman.

Zara stared around at the man and the youth, at the raging sea and at the sheer cliff. High above them, faces peered down from a platform where an aeon ago a sacrifice had been made, now rejected by Apollo. Eurycles stared into Zara's still vacant eyes, his hands searching for signs of broken limbs as he gently called her name, over and over. Eventually she saw him. She smiled.

Eurycles, Zara and Panther sat side by side on a spray-splattered rock and watched the large wooden cross being tugged out to sea. It occasionally tipped up as waves and undertow fought over it, as if waving farewell to the sacrifice it had offered to Apollo. No one spoke. They were too exhausted even to think. It was enough that they had cheated death, and if they could find the will to speculate on their fate, they might have despaired that there was no escape from their rock, no stair or pathway, and before them a furious ocean that would not give them a second chance.

It was an age before any of them found the strength to speak. Zara broke the silence — her first words in a new life.

'Is that a sail?'

The skiff had no right to survive such wild seas. Three men drew on all their experience to keep her afloat — one working the gaff-rigged sail to use the wind to keep forward motion, another the tiller to hold the small boat head on to the highest waves, and the third bailing bilge water. A fourth figure clung to the mast with one arm while signalling with the other. His keen eyes searched the stark cliff face ahead, looking for signs and landmarks he had committed to memory from his brief time among the people of Actium and their military overlords.

Ratboy knew there was little chance of finding Eurycles and Zara alive. He knew the obscure local customs and bizarre methods of sacrifice, little more than convenient methods of disposing of thieves, cutthroats and even the infirm. He had been told that he was lucky not to have gone this way himself the moment he appeared among them with a damaged leg. But both he and Shoeless had known what was in the mind of Publicola and his cruel gaolers, and they had immediately set off at a run to the fishing village. Their painful, sweaty and gut-busting sprint had been made worse by the fact that neither had footwear.

Niko had instantly grasped the issues. Two boats were needed, one to cross the straits to find Myron and *Hera* to deliver messages about the enemy's intentions, the other to search for — most likely — the bodies of Eurycles and Zara. As Niko set sail to cross the straits, Shoeless and Ratboy were waylaid by a tough fisherman with features of dark oak, formed through years of battling Poseidon's worst. The man had volunteered his small boat when Ratboy insisted the victims could be alive and would heap riches upon those that rescued them.

Ratboy still believed the impossible as he wiped sea-spray from his eyes and scoured the cliffs ahead. Behind him the fisherman, his mate and Shoeless fought to hold the boat on course, ever closer to the dangerous cliffs. The fisherman knew the place where the bodies would be — he had searched here before when he had lost a son to the cruel beliefs inspired by Apollo's murderous priests. Another reason to help these desperate southerners.

Promised riches were not important to him. Besides, he admired the lad for his unswerving faith.

Panther leapt and yelled, waving his arms as wildly as his drained energy would allow. Eurycles and Zara still could not move, but both stared across the riotous waters at the unsteady sail and calmly assured each other there could be no other reason for such bravery in these conditions than the determination of friends. A slight change of course provided further assurance that they had been spotted.

But Eurycles also knew that their rescue would be perilous among unyielding rocks and the confusion of swell and undertow. There was every chance a wave would crush the boat against their rock. Now he could see Ratboy in the bows and thanked the gods for the boy's perseverance. He counted heads — three other men, and he could tell they knew what they were doing. Panther was young; he would be all right, but Eurycles and Zara were bruised, bleeding and exhausted. Zara had defied the three-headed dog Cerberus and returned from the underworld. Eurycles felt as though he had been there too. Would the gods have allowed all this and contrived their rescue only to change their minds? Eurycles summoned resolve and gently squeezed Zara's hand.

The gnarled fisherman loosed the sail as the boat approached, riding a powerful wave to come near. He judged it perfectly as the wave's backwash slowed their progress after meeting land. Holding the free end of a fastened rope, Ratboy timed his leap as the bow crunched against rock. He slipped on weed but held on. Eurycles and Zara were on their feet now, clinging to each other, while Panther skilfully caught a second rope thrown from the stern by Shoeless. The two youths struggled to bring the boat side on but eventually it obeyed, and the gunwale grated against unyielding rock. Shoeless leapt ashore, surefooted as a mountain goat, threw strong arms around Zara and gingerly lifted her aboard. Eurycles followed before Panther jumped, just as an incoming wave lifted the boat without warning. He slipped on the wet timbers and fell between boat and rock, but strong arms caught his wrists and hauled him aboard, where he writhed like a landed octopus, clutching at his bruised and scraped shoulder and neck. Boat and rock crashed together where his head had been just a heartbeat earlier.

The boat was overcrowded now and lower in the water. A wave surged over the seaward side. The fisherman fought the sail while his mate and Shoeless tried to shove off with oars. The wind eddied at the base of the cliff, providing no certainty of direction. Eurycles crawled over Zara's body to the tiller, Panther shaking off pain and dizziness to help. Ratboy, fearlessly drawing on instinct honed from his time at sea, pushed on the sail's boom while the fisherman heaved on its sheet. A fortunate gust filled the sail and dragged them clear with sluggish forward motion.

The fisherman shouted a warning, but Eurycles had already seen the oversized wave bearing down upon them. Panther sensed the urgency and the pair coaxed the rudder, willing the skiff's prow to meet the wave head on; if it hit them abeam, they would be swamped or even capsized. Eurycles wasn't sure if he was begging Poseidon's mercy out loud. All of them were willing the boat to come about. The wave was almost upon them when Eurycles caught Zara's eye. She sat in two hand-widths of sloshing sea water, her head resting against a thwart that also served as a rowing bench, arms interlocked around her knees, watching Eurycles fighting the elements with fortitude lesser mortals could only dream of. Water streamed from her hair and beaded on her chest, which swelled with every breath.

She smiled at him as the boat began its climb, like a gull with wind beneath its wings. She did not look at the oncoming wave. Eurycles drew strength from her and did not watch the wave either. He ceased the pointless prayers. A strange calm filled his mind as he held her gaze in an impossible silence, as if even the gods held their breath.

The skiff, small and insignificant in the vastness of raging seas, bearing seven souls locked in the unity of courage and defiance, sought the summit at a perilous angle. The starboard bow met the top of the wave just as it broke. Whitewater surged at its flank and over the gunwale. The gallant skiff hesitated, pointing high to the skies where Apollo considered his final judgement.

At last the god relented. He chose life for these mere mortals.

CHAPTER NINETEEN

The two Greek seamen picked their way along a rutted road between the fleet's anchorage and Octavian's vast camp. The might of Rome was already awake. Woodsmoke curled from a thousand cooking fires in dawn's temporary respite from the unseasonal squalls that had rolled across the Ionian Sea for three days, trapping opposing fleets close to shore in their respective havens.

Only the bravest and the best took their chances on such unpredictable seas. Every day brought its perils, and Niko considered a night-time crossing in a hardy fishing vessel a risk worth taking. If what Shoeless Luka and Ratboy had told him was true — and there was every reason to believe them — he had a double purpose in staying alive. He had to deliver news that might change the course of a war, but more importantly he needed to summon Myron and the crew of *Hera* to do what they did best — rescue Eurycles or at least recover his body for a dignified crossing to the underworld. Niko was not a religious man, but like everyone he respected the gods because you never knew when you might need their help. He had needed it on the choppy straits in wind that never quite decided which way it was going to blow.

Finding *Hera* and her captain Myron had not been easy either. Threading between the ordered rows of anchored warships by moonlight, calling to their crews for news of the little Greek ship and being cursed for disturbing their sleep, he had found her moored alongside a trireme fortunate enough to have its own berth against a rocky quay. Ever diligent, Myron was awake and helped Niko aboard, found him towels and food, and forced wine upon him until he stopped shivering enough to talk. With the first fingers of dawn peeping above the distant mountains, they went to find Agrippa.

This was not an easy task. Few sentries cared about a viper brooch that purported to be the badge of office for the general's spy network, so the pair had resorted to bluff, concocting a story that Niko was a defector who had come to reveal Mark Antony's plans. Partly true, of course. And Niko looked as if he had swum across the straits to deliver his vital message. No sentry who valued his life would deny them passage and besides, what harm could two Greeks do among so many thousands of Rome's finest?

Marcus Vipsanius Agrippa's quarters, although by no means palatial, were built with sturdy pine and guarded by soldiers with the look of discipline about them. The duty *optio* knew full well what a viper brooch represented and ordered them to wait while he entered to report their arrival. Agrippa himself greeted them at the door, smiling a welcome and remembering both their names before ushering them into what appeared to be a fully functioning command centre. Tables bore large maps of the region; a secretary was already writing the day's orders by the combined light of early sun and a dozen floor-standing oil lamps. A large, contented mountain dog lay curled near a brazier of glowing embers, its oversized head immobile, although its eyes followed the newcomers as they entered, tail thumping half-heartedly on wooden floorboards. Agrippa indicated a table with benches and ordered breakfast. The secretary grumbled at the interruption to his work and made for the kitchens. Left alone, the three sat. Niko and Myron knew the appropriate etiquette and waited in silence, backs straight, arms by their sides.

'I sense you have news,' said the second most important man in Rome.

If Agrippa already knew that the Egyptian queen was planning to take flight back to Egypt, he didn't let on. There had been so many defectors since Titius and Plancus, each of them bearing news of the enemy's plans. But neither Niko nor Myron knew this. Niko blurted out the latest intelligence in excitable short sentences, making sure he played up the role of the fake priest Shoeless Luka and his accomplice, Ratboy.

'I remember the child,' said Agrippa, warming every minute to this adventurous family of scruffy but brave traders from Taenarum. 'You really should stop calling him a rat. The lad will go far and deserves a better name.'

Niko said nothing. Ratboy would always be his name.

The dog padded across the room, seeking titbits from the table. Agrippa brushed it aside and leaned forward. 'So what you are telling me is that Cleopatra wants to break through our blockade and sail back to Egypt?'

Niko chewed a large mouthful of figs and cheese, but Myron hadn't touched his platter, so he replied, 'Yes, but there's more. Apparently, Mark Antony is of the same mind.'

Agrippa raised his eyebrow — this was something he didn't know. He summoned the secretary and whispered in his ear. Myron caught the word 'Caesar' and paled. Niko, engaged with his second repast of the day, failed to grasp the significance.

Agrippa's fingers drummed the table. 'While we wait for those who need to know what you have told me, what shall we do about my friend Eurycles? You think he may have fallen victim to that bastard Publicola?'

Niko, still chewing, looked Agrippa in the eye. 'And the lady Zara too,' he said.

'Then there is no hope for them. They are dead.'

There was a moment of silence while they pondered this awful thought. The facts were plain. Niko stopped chewing and looked from Agrippa to Myron and back again. 'I will not believe that,' he said, 'not until I see their lifeless bodies. Ratboy and Luka went in search of them, and that other boy stayed close after they were taken. There's still hope.'

Myron nodded, hope hanging by a thread. 'When we are finished here, we will take *Hera* and bring them back, dead or alive.'

Again, Agrippa raised his eyebrow. 'You want to sail your ship into the wolf's lair?'

Myron wouldn't hesitate to sail into Tartarus itself to find Eurycles, and he knew Niko and the crew would willingly follow. Before he could answer, Agrippa spoke again.

'And what news of Strabo? Caesar has great affection for the writer, as do I.'

Myron looked at Niko, who shrugged and appeared to be searching his memory for the last time he saw the amiable Strabo. 'We thought he had gone to plead for his sister, the lady Zara,' Niko said hesitantly, 'but now that you ask, no, we have neither seen nor heard from him since they were taken.'

Agrippa studied the two seamen for several heartbeats, a drawn-out moment in which both realised their hitherto perfect report was flawed by the absence of one vital piece of information. But Agrippa did not approve of the angry table-thumping of many of his colleagues and sighed, almost in sadness.

'I will agree to your mission to search for Eurycles and this woman, if they live, which I think is doubtful. I will give you extra men who are skilled in dark methods of war to aid you should you encounter the enemy. But my condition is that you find Strabo or at least bring news that he is safe. Can you do this for me? For our friends?'

Myron was quietly surprised at the depth of feeling shown by this powerful Roman general. He was about to answer when the secretary returned, almost falling through the door in his hurry to announce that Caesar Octavian and two of his commanders had arrived.

A man's reputation rarely lives up to reality. Chairs scraped as the two Greek seamen stood, straightening their stained clothing. Niko ran his fingers through his thick, dark hair, while Myron cleared his throat. The dog's tail thumped on the floor.

They expected a man calling himself Caesar to be broad and powerful, with a commanding, no-nonsense presence. The man who entered was thin and in his early thirties, Myron guessed, with an almost startled look on his pale, angular face. His hair was in need of a comb, and he had long limbs, like a spider — the spider at the centre of a huge Roman web in which his rival's defecting officers had landed.

Two men followed him into the room, both of a similar age to Caesar and Agrippa. They were not like the overweight older lieutenants of Mark Antony's ranks. All three were dressed casually and their cold, grey eyes studied the two Greeks as if they had no right to be in Rome's war room.

Agrippa introduced Myron and Niko. He spared them the embarrassment of merely having single names by naming Caesar simply as 'Octavianus' and the others as fleet commanders Lucius Arruntius and Marcus Lurius. Then he told the newcomers of the news these Greeks had brought, that both Mark Antony and Cleopatra would seek to break out from their entrapment by sea, bringing a grunt of appreciation from Octavian and a warmer light to the eyes of Arruntius and Lurius.

'When?' Octavian asked.

'Local wisdom has it that the seas will calm tonight,' said Agrippa, who had sought the advice of experienced fishermen in the area. He turned to Myron. 'Would you agree?'

Three pairs of eyes appraised the Greek sea captain. Myron was not awed, confident in his own knowledge of coastal conditions. 'The signs are that yes, the winds will blow again today and will lose their power around dusk. But they will return from the north later tomorrow.'

Octavian's spider gaze held Myron on a gossamer thread of appraisal. He decided that this young seaman knew what he was talking about, then turned to Agrippa. 'Are we ready?'

'We are.'

Agrippa indicated the map table and the four Romans gathered around it, Myron and Niko standing apart, uncertain as to their role at the centre of a debate to decide the world's future, yet close enough to hear what they were saying. They felt uncomfortable but the four generals did not ask them to leave, perhaps over-eager to at last engage the enemy after months of futile skirmishes. They soon learned it was Agrippa who was the true leader in the matter of warfare at sea, drawing on his vast experience in the defeat of Sextus Pompey with a fleet of fast ships and well-trained crews. The tactics seemed obvious to Myron and Niko as they strained to see where Agrippa was pointing on the largest map. They saw the bottleneck of the straits leading out of the inner Ambracian gulf to the open seas, where the spider's web would be arrayed to catch them — Agrippa's ships on the left flank, Arruntius in the centre and Lurius and Octavian on the right.

'If what these men have told us is true,' said Agrippa, 'they will make for the centre of our lines. If they do this, Arruntius can ease back to give them confidence and our flanks can then encircle to trap them.'

'Numbers?' Octavian asked.

'We have two-hundred-and-fifty. Mostly triremes armed with harpax artillery, adapted both for grappling and fire-throwing, and many support ships. The enemy have more ships and they are bigger and slower. They will be armed with *ballistae* and scorpios and they will be manned by Antony's legions, floating fortresses bristling with archers and spearmen.'

Octavian leaned closer to the map. 'And the Egyptians?'

'Even larger ships, big enough to carry catapults to lob fireballs at us but, if the intelligence is correct, these have only one purpose and that is to flee. In which case, they will be carrying Cleopatra's treasure.' Agrippa paused, thoughtful, then added, 'If her ships are to flee south to Egypt with all this gold, they will carry their sails and wait for the afternoon winds that blow from the north.'

Usually, ships engaged in sea warfare under oar-power left their sails behind to make more room for troops on the decks. But if the enemy ships stowed their sails for flight, pursuing Roman vessels would struggle to catch them as their rowers tired, with no sails of their own.

Octavian grasped the point and suggested Rome's ships should carry their sails also to be ready to give chase, but his argument lost its force as his admirals shook their heads. Of the three generals, only Agrippa had the authority to disagree with Caesar — his tactics had won the day in the war against Sicily.

'Our priority must be to defeat Mark Antony,' he said. 'To do that, we have already cleared the decks of our triremes for soldiers and artillery. Our rowers are well-fed and trained in sea-skills, and we will outmanoeuvre the enemy's bigger ships.'

Myron was surprised to see Caesar acquiesce but also wondered why he had not been asked to de-mast *Hera*, even with harpax weapons mounted fore and aft. He got his answer as Agrippa continued.

'However, we have a fleet of small scouting ships that are capable of harnessing the wind to carry messages between us.' Now Agrippa pointed to Myron and Niko. 'Like their ship. Fast under sail with a sting like a wasp and every reason to wish to see Mark Antony defeated.'

Arruntius and Lurius nodded their approval. They had witnessed *Hera* with her unusual purple sails and astonishing manoeuvrability and speed. Even Octavian smiled his acceptance of Greek seamanship.

Agrippa hadn't finished with his praise for the plucky *liburnian* and her crew. 'However, this ship's commander is feared lost. He and his men have proved their loyalty time and again and have delivered invaluable information, as you have heard in this room today. But he has fallen into Publicola's hands, and we all know what that means.'

'Probably tortured and executed,' said Octavian. 'We should move on with the matter at hand.'

Myron and Niko bridled but Agrippa held up a hand, palm out, in a calming gesture. 'We owe Eurycles a huge debt of gratitude. These men risked their lives to extract Titius and Plancus and again more recently to provide us with vital information about Mark Antony's intentions. And they will yet play a further part in this fight.'

Arruntius, not so familiar with the background to this heroic tale, asked, 'Why so?'

Agrippa filled them in about the cruel execution of Lachares and his son's determination to seek revenge. 'Eurycles is a hero,' he said, then pointed again to the two Greeks. 'And so are these men. While there is hope that their commander yet lives, we should send them and their ship to rescue him. And if possible, we should find Strabo, who may also have fallen into the enemy's hands.'

The smallest flicker of interest crossed Octavian's cold features. 'The writer?'

'The same,' said Agrippa. 'Apparently he chose to observe this war from the wrong side of the battle lines, but for reasons I won't bore you with, we believe he is in grave danger. It will not go well for him if Publicola has captured him and makes the connection.'

'Very well,' said Octavian. 'Just one ship will be no great loss to our cause.'

Lurius, who had remained silent throughout the discussion, now made a pointed observation. 'One ship may be nothing, but we are still outnumbered by the enemy fleet.'

'True,' said Agrippa. 'What if we could even the odds?'

Everyone looked at him. 'How?' asked Octavian.

'Fire ships,' said Agrippa.

CHAPTER TWENTY

Hera slipped her moorings and left the lee of the larger trireme to brave the gusting winds that had forced Octavian's fleet to shelter for three days. Standing on the command deck, leather jerkin belted tight against the whipping wind, Myron was impatient for open seas, despite the conditions. If Niko could sail a mere fishing boat across the straits from Actium, *Hera* would easily take this mission in her stride.

'Half sail,' he ordered. No need for his fifty oarsmen to exert themselves — let the breeze do the work. These were tough, loyal rowers from Taenarum, capable warriors armed with a variety of swords, knives, axes and clubs. He had no doubt they would acquit themselves well, yet he was grateful to Agrippa for adding to *Hera*'s firepower. Two harpax weapons were mounted on the stern and bow, and there were twenty leather-clad archers armed with powerful composite bows and, for close-quarter engagement, short swords and lethal *pugio* daggers. The archers were also trained in operating the harpax *ballistae*, each capable of hurling flaming bolts at the rate of one every ten heartbeats. They were led by a wiry Etruscan with close-cropped hair and lively dark eyes who declined to be called by his Roman name. 'I am Laris,' he had announced, 'here to help you rescue a hero.' He had immediately placed his men in the ship's bows with himself foremost, as if an arrowhead seeking the enemy's heart.

Standing beside Myron on the stern command platform, Niko steered *Hera* past the outer vessels of the anchored war fleet which they now knew would soon challenge Mark Antony as the enemy sought to break out from the safety of the inner sea. Ahead of them, several coastal traders made their way slowly into the Ambracian Gulf, as ungainly and ponderous as the warships were sleek and fast, masquerading as harmless merchantmen plying their trade with no apparent threat to either side in a foreign war. But their cargo was pitch-soaked and their small crews skilled in pyrotechnics, every one of them crazy enough to embark on a one-way adventure to sow mayhem among the enemy vessels.

Agrippa's fire ships.

Myron quietly wished them the luck of the gods — they would need it — but *Hera* had a mission of her own that was equally as dangerous. She would go in fast, deploy the ship's marines if they came under attack, and get out quick. Hopefully with Eurycles and his woman, if by some miracle they had survived their ordeal at the hands of Publicola. He had his doubts, but Ratboy had believed it possible and so must he.

Hera approached the strait's southern shore about an hour before dusk. Here pine, carob and laurel jostled for space on rocky terrain close to the sea's edge, as if fleeing the invader's carpenters. Their luck held when the wind dropped and the mainsail hung loose, exactly as predicted. An eerie silence fell, in which the only sound was the music of subsiding swell lapping at *Hera*'s hull, crew and marines awed as the nearby woods seemed to draw breath. As a few birds found voice and the first tentative cicadas rasped their rhythmic refrains, Myron ordered the sail furled and the ten rowers nearest the bow to keep a slow count and a gentle forward motion.

'Easy now, count in your heads and maintain silence,' he said, just loud enough for all to hear. 'We approach enemy waters, so be ready for sudden action.' Laris and his archers were crouched in the bows, silent and watchful.

Niko steered the slow-moving *liburnian* parallel to the coast, now just a stone's throw off their starboard beam where the chorus of birds and insects swelled. They would move slowly and silently towards the inner sea and the fishing village where a few days earlier Niko and Eurycles had established their spy network's foothold near Actium. More in hope than expectation, Myron and Niko scoured the tangled woodland and rocky outcrops for signs of their friends. If any of them were still alive, especially Ratboy, they would know that *Hera* would come looking for them.

Progress was slow, stealth paramount. Dusk was near and the birds knew it, their songs fewer. Close to shore, a pair of cormorants made their last dives of the day. Niko pointed east, where smoke drifted peacefully in leaning columns, perhaps a mile away, probably the cooking fires of the fishing village. They knew that not far beyond a huge fleet would be preparing for war with thousands of soldiers massed, ready to embark on the great sea-going fortresses, artillery primed and fire braziers lit. Somehow, the new calm felt like an enormous lie.

Laris was first to spot movement on the shore. Perhaps he merely sensed a presence, but he leaned forward and peered at the woodland off the starboard bow. A hand-signal from Myron stilled the rowers and *Hera* slowed. The marines quietly picked up their bows and nocked arrows, ready for trouble — they trusted their leader who had the sharpest eyes and ears among them and was rarely wrong about danger ahead.

Ratboy stepped out from behind his cover and ten marines on *Hera*'s shoreside flank aimed deadly arrows at him. 'Hold!' Myron spat the command as a hoarse whisper loud enough for all to hear. As the marines lowered their bows, Ratboy signalled that silence was essential then pointed east, indicating a place further along the shore where they might meet in relative safety. He disappeared back into the woodland and *Hera* resumed her cautious progress. The chosen rendezvous was obvious — a small estuary leading to drying mudflats, where a small brook emptied the merest trickle into the straits, thirsting for autumn rains. On one side, tamarisks and pines fought for space, leaning precariously over the still water. Ratboy crouched on the angular trunk of a pine that reached over the deeper part of a channel, and Niko knew instinctively what the crazy youth had in mind. He steered the ship beneath Ratboy's perch and the marines watched open-mouthed as a barefoot boy dropped lithely among them, landing like a silent, grinning cat on *Hera*'s deck.

'Moor there.' Ratboy pointed to a spot opposite where brightly coloured vegetation draped itself on sheltered water. Myron was quietly pleased the youth had survived but said nothing, taking in his ragged clothing and thinking how something had changed him, made his face harder and given a boy's body a man's muscles. He beckoned and Ratboy threaded his way between rowers and their benches to the command platform.

'Well?' A simple question requiring a simple answer.

'Eurycles lives, and the lady.' Relief coursed through Myron, Niko too. 'But he is wounded and both are being cared for. They need rest, but they aren't going to get it.'

'Why is that?' Myron asked, but he knew the answer and Ratboy didn't need to tell him the enemy was close at hand. So he adjusted his question. 'Where?'

'In the fishing village.' Ratboy pointed east. 'Less than a mile over there. They are being cared for by Grandmother.' Niko knew immediately who Grandmother was — the old woman who had been impressed by Ratboy's exploit in dispatching the enemy spy and who had given them her blessing and well-wishes in the village tavern — and he told Myron that Eurycles and Zara would be suitably cared for with healing herbs and a lifetime's knowledge.

But Ratboy interrupted. 'There are soldiers there. They came down to the coast when the sun was high. They are all around. Something is happening, something big. They came to the village and took all of the fishing boats, including ours.'

Myron nodded thoughtfully. 'They need smaller boats to carry messages between their ships and the fleet commanders. They will come out at dawn.'

'Did they find Eurycles?' Niko asked. 'Were they looking for him?'

Ratboy shook his head. 'No, they don't know he is alive, and they don't care. Besides, Grandmother placed the sign of the plague on the door, so even if they search for valuables, they won't go in there.'

Myron smiled at the ingenuity, his mind racing at the prospect of a swift and stealthy rescue mission. Then he paused, remembering Agrippa's wishes.

'And Strabo? What of him?'

'The writer?' Ratboy shrugged. He had enough to think about. He couldn't even remember when he had last seen the man. He looked crestfallen, as if he had failed in his mission, so Myron came to his rescue.

'No matter. If Strabo is nearby, we will find him. But that leaves Luka. Where is he?'

Ratboy brightened. 'Shoeless and Panther watch the village from a safe distance. We knew you would come and we can show you where Eurycles and the lady are, as well as the enemy's numbers and positions.'

Myron had heard enough. He ordered the crew to begin disguising the ship with branches and foliage and summoned

Laris to join him, with Niko and Ratboy, on the shore. Ratboy was first to turn to leave, but he was held back by a strong hand on his shoulder. He turned, startled. Niko hugged him with powerful arms.

'Missed you, little runt,' said the sailor. 'You've done well.'

Ratboy blinked back tears. Passing them, Myron gave the youth a playful punch on the shoulder and winked at Niko.

'Watch out for your job,' he muttered out of the corner of his mouth. 'Looks like we've just found someone better.'

CHAPTER TWENTY-ONE

The column advanced slowly in the dead of night. Ratboy led, Laris on his shoulder, behind them the twenty marines moving silently, faces blackened, Myron and Niko bringing up the rear. A carpet of spent pine needles softened footfall, a full moon's silver light sufficient to tread around the heaviest undergrowth. No breeze, every sound amplified — the scream of an owl's prey, a fox's cough.

They had left *Hera*'s crew to guard the camouflaged ship, but they were confident the enemy would not patrol at night. Too weary, too hungry, too lazy. Yet they took no risks; the ship's crew and shore marines were focused on a single mission.

Whether Ratboy found Shoeless Luka and Panther or they found the column would be debated at length another time, but the barefoot sailor and the youth from Samos suddenly appeared from the shadows before Laris had even raised his bow. 'You make more noise than a herd of swine,' Shoeless whispered. 'Where's Myron?'

Word was passed to the marines to stand easy as *Hera*'s captain joined Laris and Ratboy to hear from Shoeless, who revealed in hushed tones the fishing village was quiet. Panther squatted next to him, tense and watchful like the wild cat that gave him his name.

'There are about thirty of the enemy remaining after some took the boats and others returned to their camp,' Shoeless reported. 'They have raided the homesteads and raped the women, but they have not found Eurycles and Zara.' At the mention of atrocities, Laris's grip tightened on his bow, his eyes grim in the shadowy light. Shoeless sensed his outrage,

161

knowing that should they be discovered, many of the enemy would die this night. He went on, 'The homesteads are arranged around an open area, where the enemy's cooking fires now burn low. These men were all drunk and are now sleeping it off either in huts they have commandeered or on the beach. There are no boats left, so we cannot leave that way.'

Myron whispered, 'Can Eurycles and his woman walk? We will have about a mile to cover back to *Hera*, possibly harassed by the enemy.'

Moonlight caught the white of Shoeless's teeth as he grinned. 'Their ordeal has been great, and both are bruised and sore. Eurycles seems pale from blood-loss. But you know him as I do, and he would even carry Zara on his shoulder if he had to.'

'Where in the village is Grandmother's hut, where they lie?' Myron asked.

'The far side from where we stand,' Shoeless replied. 'We can skirt around the edge to find them, but then it will be best to take the shortest route out, which would mean crossing the common ground without cover.'

'If I may,' Laris interrupted. 'It seems to me that perhaps two will go in and four will seek to escape the village.'

It was Panther who made the logical suggestion. Gripping the hilt of the long knife he had carried throughout a terrible ordeal — was it only yesterday? — he spoke with calm authority beyond his years. 'The two who should go in are me and Ratboy.'

There was a moment's silence as if the men present were searching for a counter argument but finding none. It made sense to all of them. The enemy soldiers were less likely to give attention to two youths than to armed marines or tough seamen. Myron nodded thoughtfully and grunted his approval. He knew and trusted Ratboy and as for this Panther, he sensed in him courage and skill. The two would go in with stealth and could defend themselves if need be.

As he mused, he felt a tap on his shoulder. It was Laris. He pointed east, where a mysterious glow reflected off low cloud far beyond the village, above the vast Ambracian gulf where Mark Antony's ships were gathered. As the men watched, the red radiance grew in intensity, casting faint reflections on upturned faces. Several exclaimed, fearing the wrath of local gods.

Myron broke the spell. 'Fire ships,' he muttered loud enough for those nearby to hear. 'Agrippa's fire ships. His plan has worked.'

Laris, more used to thinking like a land commander, snapped his fingers to draw everyone's attention back to the mission. 'If the enemy has seen this, it may give us the diversion we need. We go in as planned, with my men covering the withdrawal of your people. But we must move fast and hope this fire causes enough confusion so that the enemy does not see what we are doing.'

Grateful for the Etruscan's decisive words, Myron added, 'We go. Laris has command. Move quietly.'

Twenty marines, three Greek seamen and two youths advanced in grim and silent formation towards the village, beyond which the fires of war were stoked.

The men knelt in a line facing the village, at their centre Laris and Shoeless. Myron and Niko stood behind, deeper in the woodland cover. Each leather-clad marine carried a short composite bow, quivers of a dozen iron-tipped arrows at their shoulders, deadly knives the length of a forearm sheathed at their waists. Myron's heart raced, but he was glad of the grim company Agrippa had sent with them, silent men of steel with blackened faces, their cold eyes barely reflecting the red glow of distant fires where Mark Antony's ships burned.

'Which hut?' Laris asked Shoeless, who crouched next to him.

Shoeless pointed to a large homestead a hundred paces opposite, dimly lit by the embers of a cooking fire. An old woman sat cross-legged outside the entrance, above her a sheet of cloth nailed to the door, which he knew announced a non-existent plague.

The village was quiet. The enemy had done its worst and the villagers were subdued. Several bodies lay where they had fallen after defending their families, crumpled men bleeding out on the dry, dusty ground they once called home. Distressed keening drifted from one hut; the others were silent for fear of more vengeance. The air was thick with the pervading smell of the village's last catch before their fishing boats were stolen and their lives ruined.

Laris tensed as a man stumbled from one of the huts and urinated into open space just outside the door. He instinctively knew this was the enemy. Unsteady and probably inebriated, yes, but years in the military told him this was a soldier. Every one of his men knew it too, and all along the line bowstrings tightened. The man finished his steaming stream and looked up, seeing the glow in the east. He scratched his head, puzzled, then went back inside.

Shoeless nudged Laris and pointed to the old woman who guarded the hut where Eurycles and Zara lay. She was looking to her left, perhaps whispering. Slow-moving shadows at the edge of the homestead told them that Ratboy and Panther had arrived after circling around the village's outskirts.

Three men emerged from the hut where the soldier had urinated and looked east, pointing to the mysterious red glow which could only be caused by a raging blaze. They trotted towards the shore to get a better view, leaving the village still once again.

Shoeless and Laris silently willed the two boys to hurry; the ideal opportunity was now. They saw the youths slip into Grandmother's hut, followed by the old woman. Minutes passed, Shoeless muttering, 'Come on, come on,' until Laris nudged him quiet. The door opened and four figures emerged, moving gingerly past the cooking fire and starting across the village common, watched by Grandmother from her doorway.

The men returned from the shore, seemingly agitated, several drowsy soldiers with them. They roused their colleagues in neighbouring huts, men stumbling into the dim moonlight, looking around as if under attack before seeing the crimson cloud. Grandmother went to them. 'Don't do this,' Laris said to himself, knowing she would try to divert attention away from the small group now making its way painfully slowly across the common. Twenty bowstrings stretched, a risky longshot as the knot of soldiers was almost out of range, but these were all skilled archers.

Grandmother reached the soldiers and remonstrated with them. Her commanding voice was just audible to the men of *Hera*, but the words were lost in the night. A soldier pushed her in the chest, but she was defiant. Another struck her and she fell. 'Hold,' said Laris, just loud enough for his men to hear. Eurycles and Zara were closer now, walking unaided but slowed by injury and exhaustion. Grandmother's curses were chilling enough for the soldiers to hesitate, then one of them saw the shadows crossing the common. He peered into the gloom, then pointed, and began to stammer an alarm just as Laris's arrow took him in the chest. The others were confused for a moment before their training kicked in and they dived for cover. Three of them were too late but four others crawled behind the nearest hut, shouting their warning.

'Aim at the doorways,' Laris told his men, 'but be sure they are enemy before you loose.'

Then came Grandmother's clarion call to her people, shrill but commanding in local Greek. Her words were lost to the rescuers, but their meaning was evident — she was warning the villagers to stay inside.

The soldiers had chosen to sleep in huts close to each other, and the doors nearest the commotion were opened while other men emerged from the nearby shore. The moonlight and fire in the east were enough for Laris's men, whose night-vision had been honed on many a clandestine mission. Three soldiers died within two paces of their hut, the rest retreating indoors or rolling away to find cover. A commander's deep voice barked orders, and Laris searched for its source — he always sought to cut off the serpent's head. But he could not identify this man. Yet.

The refugees were almost upon them. The line of archers parted to allow them through. Eurycles breathlessly hailed them as he passed, Shoeless directing the four to the rear where Myron waited, and the line closed again.

As he watched for enemy movement, Laris thought quickly. The question was, would this commander whose voice he had heard consider four people fleeing an occupied village important enough for him to pursue? If they did, the numbers were now almost equal, and his men held the advantage of cover and lethal firepower. He sensed rather than saw movement and guessed the enemy soldiers were now arming themselves. His would be the advantage unless the soldiers could reach them with close-quarter sword and shield. And if they wore body armour, they would be harder to drop.

The enemy commander decided this daring escape could not go unpunished, but he foolishly chose a frontal assault. His voice rang out again and armed men poured out of the surrounding huts and away from their cover. They were easily identified — some wore a mail shirt or cuirass, and some carried a spear and shield or a short sword. All were easily distinguished from villagers, even in the dark. Eight of them were felled before they had taken three steps, those with body armour taking arrows in the neck or groin, and Laris knew the enemy's numbers were now halved.

Without taking his eyes off the battlefield, he told Shoeless to go with the others back to the ship. 'We will kill them all. Now go.' Shoeless nodded, accepting that all of the enemy must die, otherwise those left alive would doubtless burn the village.

The enemy now approached at a trot, their commander in the lead. He was a brute of a man, squat and broad-shouldered, the only one wearing a helmet. He seemed oblivious to the numbers he was losing as eight more fell wounded behind him. Laris aimed for his neck, but the arrow glanced off the crestless helm. Someone else took him in the groin. He stumbled, and Laris's second shot didn't miss its mark.

There were now only half-a-dozen, but these hesitated as rocks and stones rained on them, thrown by villagers who had seen what was happening and now came to vent their anger. Laris ordered half his men to fall back while he remained as the last of the enemy died. Stumbling through the carnage, Grandmother came, picking up a spear to finish any that still moved. She spoke firmly to the villagers, telling them to go back to their homes lest more soldiers came.

Laris stood and saluted her. 'Your people are in good hands!' he called. 'I greet you warrior to warrior.' It was the most noble compliment he could think of in the moment.

A grim half-smile was her response. 'Your work has only just begun,' she said. 'A bigger battle will follow. Rid us of these invaders and may the gods guide your arrows.' She turned to go, then looked back. 'And tell Eurycles and Zara to come back here soon, and I will bind them in marriage.'

CHAPTER TWENTY-TWO

Laris was last to return to the ship as dawn broke. He had walked backwards much of the way, his bow sweeping in a wide arc lest any of the enemy had survived and followed. Take precautions and live. Better safe than sorry.

Hungry and thirsty, he was pleased when his men passed him hard rations and a wineskin. Then he looked at the prize of a night's work in which he had lost no men. Eurycles and Zara greeted him, weak but grateful smiles on their faces. He saw the bandage on Eurycles' hand and the colourful bruises that a woollen shirt could not hide, and he knew this man had been through a barely imaginable ordeal. Zara was also weak but defiant, her striking features scratched and bruised, a shawl clasped close around her as if to ward off another blow to her dignity. Her eyes shone with new hope, creased at the corners in warm thanks. She reminded Laris of a beautiful priestess who had accepted his altar offering and touched his forehead with blessings for the mission that had brought him to this unexpected place, giving him divine protection that he would never doubt.

The crew were all at their stations, grinning at the return of their lord. Ratboy strutted on the command deck, the energy of youth willing them to depart. Panther brought Zara another cup and bade her drink. Even though she was sated with herbed wine, she surrendered gracefully in appreciation of his devotion.

Myron raised his cup. 'Men, you have all proved your worth this night,' he said. 'I am proud of you all, those who fought and those who remained to defend our ship. You are all heroes.'

A murmur of agreement swelled. All were reluctant to cheer in the expected fashion, wary that an enemy may be close at hand.

'We salute the return of Eurycles, Lord of Taenarum and true Master of this ship.' More appreciation, slightly louder.

Eurycles waved a wounded hand in denial. 'Myron is your captain,' he said, 'and I am very tired.' Zara laid her head on his shoulder. 'And so is the lady,' he added, raising laughter with a hint of bawdiness.

'In that case,' said Myron, 'we sail for Octavian's refuge and thence for home.'

That brought a loud cheer from men who had left families behind in Taenarum. But Eurycles stood and again held up a bandaged hand.

'I am not finished here,' he announced as everyone fell silent. 'Have you forgotten how my father was so cruelly murdered by Mark Antony?' He turned to gaze at Zara. 'How his men have treated this noble lady? Yes, we sail, but if we have the opportunity, will we not avenge the death of Lachares? Will we not consign to Hades the evil that has befallen our people? Do we not have the best and most noble ship ever to sail these seas and the bravest crew since that of Odysseus?'

Jaws dropped as the crew grasped his meaning.

'Are you with me?' breathed Eurycles, then louder, 'Are you with me?'

The response was a low growl growing in strength and volume, finishing with an explosion of confirmation.

'Then we sail to battle!'

Another clamour.

'Vengeance!'

Hera edged out of the narrow estuary into bright early morning sunlight. The sea was calm, to their left side the narrow straits where Octavian's fleet stirred, to the east on their right a pall of smoke hanging low over the Egyptian and Antonian fleet.

A fleet on the move. Too many ships to count. Agrippa's fire ships had been spectacular but not terminal.

'So they did not all burn,' said Myron. Next to him on the command deck, Eurycles was staring at the flotilla as it made its way under oars towards the straits and a fight to the death, the winner to rule the world. The ships were huge, great leviathans with oars spread like insect legs, each manned by hundreds of slave rowers, the steady beat of timing drums booming across still waters.

Tiny, insignificant *Hera* nosed into the Ambracian gulf, a gnat before elephants. Despite their weariness, none slept. The sight of the enemy fleet brought renewed vigour to every man, marines who had fought through the night, crew who had watched and especially Eurycles who stood with Myron on the command deck, eyes narrowed against the glare of early sun that sparkled off the calm waters of the Ambracian gulf. Behind them at the twin steering oars stood Niko and Shoeless, the latter stripped to the waist but wearing calf-length leather trews out of respect for the honoured female guest, Zara, who sat nearby with her shawl clutched tight and her head resting on a transom rail. The crew rowed at a gentle rhythm to a count in their heads perfected over months of sailing together, the ship's mainsail stowed midships between the rowers. Laris's men relaxed in the bows, close to the forward harpax, a small version of the deadly *ballista*. It was not armed, although a pile of bolts was stacked next to it. Beside these was a supply of oil-soaked cloth, ready for use when the serious fighting began. The weapon would not be used to grapple ships as large as Mark Antony's but rather to wreak havoc with flaming missiles. A second array was positioned near the steering platform.

Myron and Eurycles exchanged a look between them, the latter giving an almost imperceptible nod in silent agreement. A hand signal obeyed by Niko and Shoeless brought *Hera's* bows in a slow arc to starboard. No one questioned their captain's decision to sail directly towards the enemy fleet; in fact, heartbeats quickened to the challenge whatever it may be.

Myron knew that the enemy fleet would not consider one small ship a threat and would not even change course to investigate. *Hera* was of sleek Greek design, complete with a wayfinding eye painted on her bows so she might not even be considered an enemy. Of course, an over-excited Antonian commander might use the opportunity for target practice but would be immediately rebuked for wasting ordnance.

The enemy fleet was at least a mile distant but already daunting in its size. It was probably equal in number to Rome's fleet that would now be forming up outside the straits, but with large vessels that would tower over Agrippa's choice of triremes and *liburnians*.

'We should learn what we can about their formation and if possible identify the flagship and the positions of the Egyptians,' said Myron. 'Their signalling too, if we can. Agrippa will welcome this, but if we can track Mark Antony we can be first to attack him.'

'My thoughts exactly,' replied Eurycles.

Ratboy brought him a water skin and he drank eagerly. His hand throbbed, but he pushed the pain aside, grateful to be alive against all odds. He turned and smiled at Zara, realising she was watching him. He knew he should get her to safety, but equally he was certain she would object to such special treatment. He also knew she shared his lust for vengeance. He took the skin to her.

'We're going to find out what we can, then return you to shore,' he said as he squatted beside her.

She gave him a look that was half amused and half defiant. 'Put me ashore? You would have to tie me up first,' she said. 'I go where you go. These brave men have risked their lives for us, and while there's breath in my body I will fight beside you.'

'But you're exhausted and hurt. You need to rest in a safe place.'

She shook her head. 'We can sleep when we're dead.'

Eurycles gently laid his forehead against hers. 'So you disobey me?'

She laughed, pushing him away. 'You have a lot to learn, Eurycles.'

They realised the crew had stopped rowing and were looking at this extraordinary pair. They cheered, bringing blushes from Zara and a rebuke from Eurycles, then resumed their work.

Hera set a course cutting across the foremost ships of the approaching Antonian fleet. There were countless warships powered by banks of rowers, at least six per oar in the larger vessels. On most of them, towers four times the height of a man had been mounted fore and aft to enable archers to shoot downwards onto the massed decks of an enemy ship, or even to support small catapults for greater range with rocks and fireballs. The fleet was imposing and frightening, but slow. In a chase, it was no match for a faster ship like *Hera* or Agrippa's new navy.

Myron pointed to one of the leading ships around which several small messenger boats busied themselves like worker bees in the hive. Twin banks of oars rose and fell methodically, and on its deck were towers painted sky blue and edged with gold. Similarly coloured pennants flew from a lavish stern pavilion.

'That must be Antony,' said the captain. 'Looks like a flagship to me.'

Eurycles made a mental note of everything about the ship, from its aggressive bronze ramming beak to the massed ranks of legionaries on the upper deck and on the towers. They could see the outline of a catapult on the foremost tower, its throwing arm pointing upwards in salute to the gods of war. A spiral of thin smoke drifted from the charcoal braziers that would set each fireball aflame to hurl at Rome's ships. Mark Antony had come to fight, whether he planned to flee or not. Perhaps he aimed to take down as many as possible in his bid to break through Octavian's line. As they came closer, they could see green weed clinging to the flagship's hull, grown there in the months of neglect while Mark Antony pontificated. It would probably slow every ship in the enemy fleet.

'So where are the Egyptian ships?' Eurycles asked no one in particular.

Myron whistled above the heads of the rowers to the men crouched forward, nearest the bows. Ratboy, as ever, was first to look up. He was beckoned and came running, skipping lightly between the rowing decks and receiving good-natured rebukes from the men whose timing he interrupted. He stood, grinning, before his captain.

'Shin up the mast,' said Myron. 'Look beyond those that approach and tell us what you see.'

The exhaustion that had built during the rescue mission fell away in a surge of teenage energy. Ratboy turned and ran back the way he had come, evoking more curses from the rowers, and grasped the hemp halyard that slapped against the mast. Gripping with his feet, he hauled himself skyward. Then, with his left arm around the tip of the mast and his right hand shading his eyes from the glare of the morning sun, he gazed east beyond Mark Antony's fleet. 'I see them!' he shouted to Myron, then hesitated as if counting the distant ships. Counting anything was not Ratboy's greatest talent.

He returned to Myron, everyone on the command deck expectant. 'There are more ships,' he said, 'a long way off, but they are also very big.'

'How many?' Myron's question furrowed Ratboy's brow.

Myron held up both hands, fingers extended. 'If this is ten, how many more are there?'

The lad thought for a moment, then extended his hands and flashed all fingers five times.

'So at least fifty, maybe sixty,' sighed Myron. 'Well done, boy. That'll do — stand down.'

Ratboy puffed out his chest at another job well done and returned to the marines in the bows.

Myron turned to Eurycles. 'It fits with what we know. Mark Antony will seek to break through the lines so that the Egyptians can flee with their treasure.'

'Good,' replied Eurycles. 'But we also need to identify Publicola's ship. We have plenty of unfinished business.'

They had already passed in front of many of the enemy's foremost ships, but Zara, now gripping the stern railings, did what only a woman who knew her enemy could do.

'I see him.'

'Where?' Eurycles demanded. His eagerness for retribution was equally as hot.

Zara pointed to a ship they had already passed. A lone officer stood in the bows of a vessel slightly smaller than most of the enemy leviathans. They could make out a crested helmet; its wearer had one foot on the foremost thwart of the ship he commanded. He was probably looking directly at *Hera*, like a buzzard eyeing carrion.

'How do you know?' Eurycles asked, gently.

'I just do. I feel it, I know it.'

Myron ordered *Hera* about and soon they were making a course directly towards the suspect ship, Eurycles noting everything about the vessel — from the colours flown from a single mast to the charring along one flank, indicating a close brush with Agrippa's fireships. As they closed, it was clear that this ship had only one archers' tower; the space forward that would have been taken by a second tower contained a strange contraption that held aloft a cage made of sturdy canes. Within this cage was an animal. Or a man, slumped disconsolately in cruelty's evil grip.

Hera slowed, not daring to come too close. A signal from the officer on the enemy ship brought archers to the nearest flank. A fight now would bring needless casualties for both crews. The officer removed his helmet, revealing short, greying hair.

'It's him,' Zara exclaimed.

Eurycles looked across the short expanse of water at his torturer, reigniting a deep, throbbing pain that shot from his mutilated hand to his shoulder.

The officer cupped his hands to his mouth. 'Who dares to come close to the rightful heirs of Rome's glory?'

Everyone fell silent, the archers on the enemy ship aiming at *Hera*, the Greek ship's marines doing exactly the same at their opponent. Laris, in *Hera*'s port bow, called to Myron without taking his eye from the officer upon whom his arrow was fixed. 'I can take him any time you want.'

A barked command brought a flurry of movement on the decks of the enemy ship. Three archers came to stand below the cage, arrows nocked and pointing upwards to the caged victim who now stood unsteadily, fists closing around the upright canes, peering at the newcomer. Naked but for a stained loincloth, his stocky body was grimy and bloodied.

'Strabo!' gasped Zara. 'They have my brother!'

Eurycles felt all the exhilaration of their escape from death drain from his soul. He paled and knew he must fight.

The officer called again. 'Who are you, Greek intruder?'

They knew this man was Publicola. Eurycles and Myron looked at each other. What to do? What to say?

Eurycles was about to answer with venomous words when Zara interjected. 'Back off, beloved. They will surely kill him before we come close.'

The man who had defied torture and death spoke in a commanding voice. 'I am Eurycles, whom you sacrificed to Apollo. But the god did not accept your sacrifice. I and the lady stand before you now, and we will send you across the Styx to find your own judgment for your wicked crimes.'

Publicola threw back his head and laughed.

'Little man, just how will you achieve this?'

Eurycles said nothing. He just turned to his left, looked at Laris and nodded.

The arrow thudded into the superstructure in front of where Publicola stood. As it quivered there, a second arrow followed, but a shield was thrust before the Antonian general to deflect the shot. Other soldiers came to form a protective wall.

Laris called, 'I was aiming for his manhood, but the target was too small!'

No one laughed.

But Publicola was not finished. 'I offer an exchange,' he called across the short distance. 'My prisoner for you and the woman. We can do this here and now.'

'Row back!' ordered Myron before Eurycles or Zara could respond.

Laris was still watching this man for whom he now felt an almost uncontrollable hatred. He looked across the barbed iron tip of his arrow and could see little to aim at, but maybe, just maybe.

He loosed.

The arrow took Publicola in the knee, just above the bronze greaves he wore on his shins, maiming him for the rest of his life — however short that might be.

Now *Hera* was turning away from the enemy, and even at half rowing speed was faster than any of the encroaching ships could match.

Zara was weeping silently. 'Dear brother,' she whispered. 'Dear brother, I have found you and lost you.'

Eurycles put an arm around her shoulder. 'He is not lost. While there is breath in my body, we will come back for him. Mark my words.'

A hail of arrows swarmed in the air above the little Greek ship as she retreated. Shieldless, and ducking beneath any cover they could find, two of Laris's marines took arrows in the throat and chest, and three stalwart rowers choked and clutched at the black-feathered shafts that struck their muscled torsos.

Myron cursed and ordered a burst of renewed speed, away from enemy shafts and towards the safety of Rome's protective fleet. But everyone on that ship knew that the day's ordeal was not over.

CHAPTER TWENTY-THREE

Tidal flow of any kind was so rare in Greek waters that it had never been of any concern to Myron. Yet now he sensed an unusual head-on current as the moon goddess Artemis summoned Ionian waters through the narrow straits to fill the Ambracian basin and cause the rowers to redouble their strokes. *Hera* carried wounded men in urgent need of a surgeon's skills, and now the gods were against them. He looked astern, where the Antonian fleet seemed motionless, perhaps hindered by the same current or aground in the shallows, distant ghosts in the shimmering mid-morning haze. Again he turned his gaze ahead, where an expanse of shallow sea now fought their progress as they sought to reach the safety of Octavian's refuge.

One dead, four wounded. Laris's men, grim-faced, laid their fallen comrade on the deck near the bows and folded his lifeless arms around weapons now clutched to his chest in preparation for his crossing. Zara tended the wounded, while Ratboy and Panther made themselves useful by bringing bandages and buckets of clean seawater. Not one of the wounded cried out when ugly arrowheads were cut or plucked from taut, inflamed flesh, aided by the strong spirit volunteered from Shoeless's secret supply.

Myron saw Zara's agonised look and knew that more would die. She worked fast, her skilful fingers staunching the flow of blood as she calmly told her young assistants where to place bandages and spoke soft words of encouragement to her patients. Eurycles came to her side and, seeing how sweat ran into her eyes, gently mopped her brow. She frowned when she saw fresh blood oozing through the crude bandage that bound his wounded hand.

'We must find respite,' she said without slowing in her work. 'How far from the shore are we?'

Eurycles stood and summoned Myron. 'How far to Octavian's haven?' he asked.

Myron studied the untroubled sea ahead, then looked at his rowers, who must surely tire soon. 'There's no breeze to speed us and unless this current relents, two hours, maybe more.'

'Twice that for Antony's fleet, I'd guess. We should rest. We need to find the nearest land, find shade for the wounded and, if possible, take on fresh water.'

Myron nodded his agreement, then pointed towards the gulf's northern coast. 'Agrippa's maps showed an island over there,' he said. 'There are hazardous shallows, but his scouts reported many salt pans and fishing nets, and the stench of garum. So I'm thinking that if they have supplied Octavian's cooking pots these past months, they will be friendly towards us and may offer us respite.' He indicated Eurycles' bloodied hand. 'And you need fresh bandages for that, old friend.'

Hera approached the island slowly. Ratboy was in the bows, peering into clear shallows to shout warnings of any dangerous rocks or mudbanks. Startled shoals of small fish darted away from the encroaching vessel while squid, eels and octopus vied for cover, rich pickings at any other time. They passed between vast nets set on poles to catch the shoaling fish, Shoeless shouting friendly greetings to fishermen who stood shoulder-deep to sieve their glittering catches into floating baskets. They saw no threat from the bearded, bare-chested seaman whose colourful Greek dialect struck a familiar chord.

Ratboy found the channel that led to a stone quay that served as the island's harbour. To make space for the visitor, skinny children pulled aside small boats that crowded the quayside like ducks squabbling for crusts of bread; all warships carried interesting things like weapons and plunder, perhaps even brave captains with tales of sea monsters and furious battles against the enemy, whoever they may be. Small hands caught the mooring ropes tossed by Ratboy in the bow and Niko in the stern, and *Hera* was secured just as her keel nudged shingle below.

The village itself was unspectacular. Flimsy huts clung to the rocky island with its sparse vegetation, clearly a summer outpost for the supply of salt and the fermented fish seasoning, garum, so much in demand when a Roman army was camped nearby. With no breeze, the smell was overpowering. A huddle of ancient carob and fig trees grew nearby, providing shade for a few goats.

An old man led around twenty inquisitive villagers to the quayside, mostly men as the island served as a simple supply operation intent on maximising summer production before the weather closed in. They approached cautiously. This was, after all, a Greek warship manned by tough oarsmen and seasoned warriors who could swiftly overwhelm their small community. Diplomacy was their only choice. If they were lucky there might be coin to be bargained for, a bonus to add to what had already proved to be a profitable season.

The villagers crowded the quay to peer at the newcomers. All were stripped to the waist — clothes were clearly an afterthought in this remote outpost — dark-skinned, lean and barefoot. Their leader was bald with an unkempt grey beard and piercing dark eyes that showed a hint of amusement until he saw the wounded men, spilt blood in the ship's bilges and the now-shrouded marine's body. And there was a woman among these fighting men — that struck him as unusual, but these were strange times and he had no understanding of Roman ways except that they paid handsomely for garum and salt. He held his arms wide in welcome and addressed the men on the command deck.

'Do you come in peace? You do not look like Romans, yet you have been at war.'

As captain, Myron answered, 'This is a Greek ship and you are Greeks, are you not? We carry two nobles who have escaped persecution, but another remains imprisoned...' He pointed vaguely in the direction of Mark Antony's fleet. 'So we must fight, but we have one dead and four severely wounded, so we seek your help.'

'Who fights who is a mystery to us,' said the headman, 'but we will help our fellow Greeks. We have remedies for your wounds and food for your men. You may choose what to eat, as long as it's fish!'

Myron bowed. 'Our thanks to you. And water?'

'We have a plentiful well, although the water is brackish. You'll get used to it.'

The wounded were helped ashore first, fussed over by Zara. Irksome flies found the scent of blood more interesting than the racks of fish drying in the sun. A girl with large brown eyes and matted hair grasped Zara's hand and led her and the walking wounded to the shady trees while small boys shooed away the goats, the scrawny animals' neck-bells chiming discordantly with their bleating protests. Ratboy and Panther were ordered to liaise with the headman for food and water, while the crew and marines were told to rest while they had the opportunity. Another child brought a bowl of foul-smelling paste to Zara, telling her it was for healing. Zara sniffed it. The heavy odour of mashed fish meal made her retch, but she thought she could also sense some sweet herbs and perhaps honey in the sticky concoction. She looked into the child's eyes and decided to trust her.

Later, Eurycles sought Zara where she tended the wounded in the trees' shade. He sat and studied her face, noticing dark shadows beneath her eyes and new worry lines around her mouth. Gently, she unwrapped the bandage from his left hand, washed the inflamed wound where rusty pincers had removed a finger, and laced it with the last of the fishy paste.

'Who knows, this magic may grow you a new finger,' she said as she bound the hand with a clean cloth. 'Otherwise you'll never be able to count to ten again.'

'That's so funny,' said Eurycles, managing a small laugh through his exhaustion. 'It's a shame there isn't any magic for that oversized nose of yours.'

She punched him playfully on the shoulder and then suddenly they were in each other's arms, kissing with a passion that shouldn't have been possible for two such bruised and battered bodies. They were only parted when the medicine child sniggered, offering them honey cakes and a warm smile.

'Archon wants to see you,' the girl said.

Eurycles knew that "archon" was probably an over-inflated term for the village headman. 'Take us to him,' he said.

'He's here,' the girl smirked, and a bald man with a beaming smile appeared from behind the carob tree. He sat on the ground opposite them and offered a spouted jug as the girl skipped away to a new adventure. For a few moments, the three drank the wine of friendship and watched the smoke drifting lazily from the dead marine's funeral pyre, grateful that none of the wounded had succumbed to Charon's summons.

The headman looked at Eurycles. 'You will go to war soon?'

Eurycles sighed wearily. 'Soon, yes. We are grateful for your kindness.'

'Your wounded men cannot go; we will care for them here.'

'And we will recompense you.'

The headman smiled and passed the wine jug to Eurycles to seal the deal. 'I do not understand these Romans who fight each other. We have prospered while they have been here, but now we want them all to go away.'

'They will be gone soon,' said Zara. 'They will destroy each other's ships and those that are left will sail away. Their legions will go somewhere else to fight and you will be left in peace.'

'No one will win,' the headman said knowingly. 'But if there's more that we can give to help you, we do so gladly.'

'You have given us food and water,' replied Eurycles, 'but can you give us fire for our weapons and wind for our sails?'

The headman pointed to the pyre, where the smoke was now beginning to spiral away to the south and the flames were finding renewed vigour. 'There is your wind and your fire. The wind will blow until darkness falls, and our fires burn long.'

The three stood and watched the smoke as it curled across the inner sea, then turned their faces to the east. The sun, at its day's zenith, shone bright on sparse clouds that rode Boreas's gentle breeze from the north, dispersing the morning's misty haze. It also scattered the peace and tranquillity that moments before had settled on Eurycles and Zara as they held each other in the shade of a carob tree.

Spread wide across the Ambracian gulf, Mark Antony's fleet was moving. It was slow and ponderous as before, with no sails yet hoisted, but it definitely grew larger as they watched.

Eurycles clutched Zara's hand. 'This is it,' he whispered. 'You must stay here in safety, and we will return for you on the morrow.'

Zara let go of his hand and glared at him. 'We've had this conversation. Do you not listen? You want me to remain on this island while my brother is held like a caged animal on one of those ships? You think that a woman cannot go to war? You men have made this mistake before.'

Eurycles touched her gently on the cheek and the fire in her eyes subsided.

'I had a feeling that would be your answer,' he said. 'Come, we have a fight to win and your brother to rescue.'

He summoned the men to a council of war.

CHAPTER TWENTY-FOUR

'What have we here?'

Marcus Vipsanius Agrippa narrowed his eyes and studied the small *liburnian* making good speed out of the Ambracian gulf's bottleneck straits. The rise and fall of her oars indicated some urgency, and her purple sails swelled with the stiffening northerly. He turned to the watch officer standing next to him.

'Taenarum's finest, if I'm not mistaken.'

Since the early alarm had sounded, he had spent the morning arranging Rome's two-hundred-and-fifty ships in crescent formation off Actium, facing the gulf's entrance. It was a blockade to face down the enemy as they emerged — those that had survived his fireships. Now he would let them throw themselves on this sea-net of firepower and escape if they could.

Agrippa had expected Antony's fleet but instead this solitary Greek ship emerged. A rueful smile crossed his face. Would that all of his crews showed the same courage and bore the same luck as these crazy Greeks. They had embarked on a suicide mission and now they were back, and it wouldn't surprise him if they had succeeded.

'Signal the fleet to hold position,' he ordered. A *cornicen* sounded a single base note, which floated on the breeze across from Agrippa's position on the left flank facing the gulf's exit straits. It was answered by the horns of Arruntius in the centre and distant Lurius, positioned with Octavian on the right. He turned to his captain. 'Good, now advance in front of the line. And show that ship my banner.'

Minerva edged forward two lengths in front of her neighbours' ordered lines of triremes and *liburnians*, three deep, the larger vessels bearing single towers painted red for easy identification in the mayhem that was sure to follow. None had brought masts and sails, allowing space for harpax *ballistae* and catapults and squads of marines and archers. Slightly larger than most in his fleet, Agrippa's flagship now held its position while the ship's *signifer* climbed the tower to wave the general's banner. Moments later, *Hera* changed course and made for *Minerva*.

Agrippa admired the ship's sleek lines as she approached, her crew adjusting the sail so that *Hera* heeled a little, white-water spuming around the bronze ramming beak at her prow. Now he could make out the knot of men on her stern platform — could that be Eurycles back from the dead? He could definitely see Myron, the solid, dependable ship's captain, and with him no doubt those unpolished gemstones, Niko and half-clothed Luka. But wait — a woman too? Her dark hair streamed in the sea breeze, her shift and cloak held taut around her body. And there in the bows, clinging to rigging like chattering monkeys, were two youths admiring the awesome sight of Rome's navy arrayed before them.

He quietly commanded his officer to have the men ship oars on the starboard side to allow the smaller vessel to come alongside, knowing that Myron and his Greeks would display deft seamanship to align the vessels perfectly. He was not disappointed. *Hera* approached in a smooth arc in front of the fleet, fire pots trailing thin smoke, flapping sail dropped expertly, port-side oars retracted at the last minute as she faced back towards the straits to nestle expertly alongside Agrippa's flagship, which provided mooring ropes fore and aft. Eurycles called for the salute, and a hundred gruff voices hailed the general. Agrippa smiled and returned a Roman salute, right fist thumping his light leather cuirass — he knew better than to wear bronze at sea, unlike some of his fellow generals. He looked down at *Hera*'s decks. The rowers looked fresh, and he was pleased to see Laris and his men poised, alert and focused in the bows, the one exception being that cheeky Ratboy character. His gaze wandered to the stern platform and that striking woman standing with Eurycles. Even the livid bruising on her face, shoulders and legs could not detract from her beauty, and whatever ordeal she had endured seemed to have failed to dissuade her from Amazonian intent. Eurycles, too, looked as if he had suffered a *flagrum* whipping, and Agrippa noted a heavily bandaged hand. But Rome's naval mastermind wasn't here to express sympathy.

'Hail Eurycles, hail men of Taenarum, hail Laris.' He raised his voice above the clamour of gulls and the sounds of a fleet positioning for battle. 'What news of Antony and the Egyptians?'

Eurycles came closer to the rails and looked up at the man he had befriended in his hometown. He was surprised by how fresh and alert Agrippa seemed after months of campaigning on land, in contrast with his own plight. He was conscious of how dishevelled he must appear to these disciplined Romans. He was about to report when a murmuring began among the bigger ship's crew. Agrippa looked around questioningly, but Eurycles saw it first. An arrowhead of geese was flying south, honking noisily. He instinctively knew what the omen meant.

'The gods confirm what Myron has previously told you,' Eurycles said. 'When Mark Antony's ships come through that gap, they will make for open seas and the Egyptians with him.'

Agrippa nodded slowly. 'But first they will fight?'

'They will have to. You have formed this wall through which they must force their way. The numbers are even and they are ready to make war. Their ships are large but hindered by weed and worm rot, and therefore slow — prime targets for your machines, your rams and your archers. They too are armed with catapults, and their braziers are alight. We have already felt the sting of Publicola's arrows.'

'It seems you have fought hard and for that Caesar is grateful,' Agrippa said. 'When you have told us what you have seen that will soon come against us, you can rest in our camp on dry land.'

Zara shook her head, Niko and Shoeless snorted in unison and Myron gave a wry smile.

'We will not rest,' replied Eurycles. 'We have scores to settle, because Mark Antony murdered my father and we have suffered cruelly at the hands of Publicola. And we have found Strabo, who is held in a cage on Publicola's ship so that if you fire upon him, the prisoner will surely die. Put us at the foremost position in your fleet, where we can avenge ourselves on these monsters.'

Agrippa seemed momentarily taken aback by this news about Strabo. 'You shall have your wish, but I will not have a single ship acting of its own volition. You will stay close to us. When Antony appears, the fleet will pull back in the centre to draw him on so that our wings can enfold him and destroy him. You will be on the left wing with me. We will harry the enemy, disable their ships, board and capture them if we can. And if it be possible, rescue Strabo. Do you still have weapons to help me do this?'

Eurycles tugged at an earlobe. 'We have two harpax *ballistae* with bolts and fire, but no grappling irons.'

Agrippa held up a hand. 'Your ship is too small for boarding bigger ships. Use fire and Laris's archers.'

Indicating the Etruscan and his archers, Eurycles replied, 'These men have served us well, and have this day lost a man with more wounded. They are all heroes but are short of arrows now after a night of fighting.'

Agrippa turned to his officer with a terse command to bring arrows from the reserve stores. Several bound bundles were passed down to Laris's men along with a box of pitch-soaked cloths to be used to shoot fire on the enemy ships. The archers eagerly stored the fresh ammunition as if they were receiving plundered gold and gems. Laris saluted but Agrippa had already turned back to Eurycles for more information.

'Now, tell me more about their ships,' he said. Even the smallest detail could make a huge difference.

With Myron's help, Eurycles recounted everything he could recall about the enemy fleet, describing Mark Antony's flagship and the colours he flew, and how the enemy had brought sails to the coming fray and therefore fewer archers and spearmen. He related the numbers of blue towers and the weaponry they bore, towers that could be dismantled and discarded overboard when the time came to hoist sails and flee. He described Antony's ship as a giant 'six' with more men per oar than any Rome had mustered; other ships in his line were equally as huge, yet even these were dwarfed by the Egyptian vessels that would come after them. Officers and crew on *Minerva* craned to hear these details, and a secretary wrote furiously on a tablet. This information would be disseminated via the many skiffs nearby, ready to take orders to the other fleet commanders.

Even as he completed his report, a stirring could be sensed in the nearest ships and a horn sounded, swiftly taken up by *cornicines* across the line. Everyone on *Minerva* turned landward, and the entire crew on *Hera* stood to crane their necks towards the inevitable. Emerging ponderously into open seas from between the twin promontories of the Ambracian straits, stark in the harsh sunshine, were the great vanguard warships of Mark Antony's fleet.

The enemy had come.

CHAPTER TWENTY-FIVE

Small boats scurried among the Roman ships bearing messages from Agrippa, and returning with responses from Octavian, Lurius and Arruntius. In front of the fleet, a forest of masts was gathering at the mouth of the straits, none yet bearing sails, closely packed but with enough space to avoid a clash of oars. Smoke from their numerous fire braziers swirled lazily around them, shielded from the breeze by the hilly coast behind them. On the southern promontory a distant clamour arose to greet the emerging fleet where Mark Antony's legions, those that had not been chosen to fight at sea, had gathered to watch like spectators in a vast arena. Swords clashed on shields, horns sounding a cacophony of notes.

On the northern promontory the ordered ranks of Rome's land army watched in silence, save for spasmodic barked orders that carried across the half-mile of open water to where *Hera* had joined the left flank of ships commanded by Agrippa. Three siege catapults had been manoeuvred onto the shingle beach, and at each shouted order the distinct clack-clack-clack of ratchets heightened the tension, even though Mark Antony would be unlikely to allow his ships within range.

Eyes shielded against the glare, Eurycles and Myron were searching the massed enemy for Mark Antony's flagship when the first shots were fired. From the near shore a loud crack was followed by a whistling as a boulder arced lazily towards the nearest ships. It fell well short in a cascade of foam. *Probably a rangefinder*, thought Eurycles. *Don't bother to fire back unless the enemy decides to fan out across a nearer shore.* However futile, it had the effect of stiffening resolve, and the throats of thousands of sailors and marines poured forth a challenge that rolled across the narrowing stretch of water between the opposing fleets. Even as the growl swelled to a roar, a second boulder was released from a larger catapult armed with a slingshot mechanism. This missile came closer, plunging not two spear-lengths from a flanking warship and sending spray across her decks. The roar turned to cheers. The drenched ship steered away from the threat, and Mark Antony's rowers seemed to redouble their efforts. The enemy came steadily on, still grouped close and forming what appeared to be an arrow formation.

Horns sounded — Agrippa's pre-arranged signals, combined with the flag and frantic hand-signalling from the *signifer* atop *Minerva*'s tower. A response sounded from Arruntius in the crescent's centre, which began to slowly edge backwards, rowers pushing rather than pulling. Perhaps this was to demonstrate fear, or encourage the enemy to hold its formation and sail into a deadly trap.

Eurycles was watching Agrippa's *Minerva* for the signal that he knew would soon come. 'Looks like the plan is working,' he said from the corner of his mouth to Myron, the steady, unflappable captain at his side.

'We'll be waiting here until all are out in the open,' replied Myron. 'And you might like to know I've found Mark Antony.' He pointed to the centre of the advancing force, Eurycles following the direction of his finger and finding there the familiar outline of his arch-enemy's flagship, its two blue-and-gold towers unmistakable. It seemed barely troubled by the open sea's swell, its banks of oars rising and falling to a deep drumbeat. Men swarmed on her decks and on the towers, arming catapults and *ballistae*, as they did on all of the approaching ships. More than a hundred enemy ships had emerged from the inner sea, and still they came.

Still watching for the signal to move, Eurycles said tersely, 'When we close the trap by encircling them, make for Antony, no matter what our orders are. We can always say we missed the signals in the heat of battle.'

'Agreed.' Myron could only guess at the confusion that would follow as the ships engaged. 'But much depends on whether the Egyptians will continue to hang back.'

Eurycles saw the point. If Agrippa encircled Mark Antony's ships before the Egyptian behemoths emerged, they themselves could become trapped with enemies in front and behind. But Agrippa had waged sea warfare before, while he hadn't. Eurycles was therefore content to leave that kind of problem to Octavian's admiral. He was more concerned with retribution and this battle would give him the perfect opportunity.

'Can you see Publicola?'

Myron shook his head. 'Perhaps on the far side? Or maybe holding back with the Egyptians to see how the battle unfolds?'

'I wouldn't put it past that opportunist snake,' muttered Eurycles.

An eerie calm replaced the early cacophony of signal horns and massed voices as the centre under Arruntius continued its slow backward retreat. The enemy's sluggish advance meant that some ships crowding through the narrow straits had fanned left and right, a few inadvertently straying within range of the shore battery. The three catapults had already been winched tight. Myron nudged Eurycles and pointed; an observant seafarer, he had seen the danger into which several ships had strayed.

All three loosed at the same moment. While the missiles seemed to float ominously in a cloudless sky, Eurycles found himself wondering what it must be like to be on a crowded deck and watch helplessly as a heavy boulder plummeted down. There would be nothing you could do but trust that the gods had chosen someone else to die this day.

Two narrowly missed the nearest target, plunging harmlessly into the depths. But one crashed through the midship superstructure, crushing men and splintering deck planking before continuing down through rowers' benches and into the bilges. It made a fatal hole in the unfortunate vessel below the waterline. The shrieks and cries of dying and mangled men could be heard in the few seconds before the triumphant cheers of Romans both on the shore and at sea. The stricken ship slewed and began to settle. Men threw themselves overboard lest another rock would plunge from the skies. The nearest ships immediately changed course in an attempt to avoid the same fate. Reloading the great shore machines would take time, but these ships were tortuously slow and when the next salvo came, they were just clear of the killing zone. However, there was further cost as one collided with its neighbour, its ramming beak shattering oars and scraping along an entire flank. They, too, floundered — three ships effectively taken out before the lines of two navies had even closed.

The Roman cheers turned to laughter.

'It's just three ships,' said Myron, now warming to his role as a captain in what could become the greatest sea battle since the war with Carthage. 'We'll have to destroy a lot more than that.'

'Not long now,' replied Eurycles. He had seen the enemy's arrow formation increase speed both to allow more ships to pass though the straits and to attack Octavian's centre, commanded by Arruntius. Their fires had been stoked and were fanned by the sea breeze, creating a heat-haze above each ship as they advanced. Eurycles looked across to see the centre still in retreat, drawing the enemy on. At *Minerva*'s command deck, Agrippa and his officers watched their scheming unfold perfectly.

Or so they thought.

CHAPTER TWENTY-SIX

In all this time of waiting and suspense, *Hera*'s crew had been patient. The rowers could see little, seated with their backs to the first exchanges in the sea battle. They had little expectation of survival. Shoeless Luka paced back and forth on the command deck, fists bunched and muttering curses to anyone who would listen. He was wearing only leather trousers cut to calf length. Niko, however, was clothed in trousers, a shirt and an oiled leather vest that stank of fish. Zara watched the enemy through narrowed eyes, ignoring the throb of her bruises and tired limbs. In the bows, Ratboy clung to rigging and watched open-mouthed as the enemy closed. Next to him, Panther checked and rechecked the sharpness of his long dagger. Both youths seemed no more than street urchins, but their blood was up, ready to do all that was asked of them and more. Laris whistled a tune, his bow placed to hand beside him with a fresh stock of arrows, occasionally smiling grimly at his men. He had never seen them so ready for action, even after such a long night of skirmishing and a morning in which they had lost men to Publicola's onslaught.

Hera might be a small ship, but she and her crew strained every sinew to show the world what she was made of. She was ready for revenge, and her crew was braced for destruction. If the gods rewarded bravery, paeans would be written about them. They had achieved much but their task was unfinished, and they all backed Eurycles and his ship's captain, Myron.

So when the command was given to advance, *Hera* danced ahead, eager to be first to spring the trap. It was not her fault that she was the fastest in the Roman fleet. Eurycles glanced back at *Minerva* and tried to read the expressions on the faces of Agrippa and his officers, but they had more to concern them than a rebellious Greek ship. Myron merely shrugged. 'Either we do this or we hang back and let these Romans take all the praise,' he said.

Eurycles gave him an encouraging slap on the shoulder, then turned to face the men at the oars. 'You are the true heroes this day, whatever happens next. Apollo has given us his approval — now let us see if Poseidon agrees.'

The men did not break stroke as they grunted affirmation. In the bows, Laris, Ratboy and Panther had stoked the fire pots that hung over the starboard and port quarters, trailing their smoke and ready to fuel fire arrows and harpax bolts. Every man was armed with a bow, spear, dagger or short sword. Zara had found herself a long-bladed dagger, craftily located by Ratboy, and she was ready to use it. Niko and Shoeless had their fists and would use their teeth if necessary, but they needed both hands to control the deep steering oars that now ploughed a furrow behind them. In the central walkway, *Hera*'s renowned purple mainsail lay ready for rapid hoisting when the wind was favourable and a burst of speed was required.

The courageous little ship went to war.

Agrippa's plan had been to close the net around Mark Antony's fleet as they advanced towards the centre of the retreating crescent. It appeared to be working. But Eurycles still worried that as yet there was no sign of the Egyptian ships. These carried much treasure, enough to pay all of Mark Antony's legions, and would surely be worthy of capture. But where were they? Agrippa seemed not to care; he was unable to resist the opportunity to surround and engage his enemy.

So *Hera* surged towards the centre of the enemy fleet to where a ponderous flagship commanded by the murderer of

Eurycles' father lay, making its steady course towards the Roman centre.

'Come to starboard, hoist mainsail.' Myron's command was immediately obeyed, and the distinct purple sail was run up the mast as Niko and Shoeless leaned into the steering oars, the sail filling and giving the ship a sudden kick of renewed energy. She surged towards the enemy under sail and oar.

'Arm both harpax. Archers stand by,' snapped Myron.

The allocated teams winched both *ballistae* taut and held bolts wrapped with pitched cloth ready to light from the fire braziers. But the enemy was ready. The first blazing fireballs launched from the nearest enemy ship to arc lazily towards the oncoming Romans. Ratboy and Panther, with other crew members, used roped buckets to haul seawater on board, ready for any enemy success with their fire weaponry. None of the missiles struck their targets, falling well short in clouds of steam. But every ship's crew knew more would follow, and those experienced in warfare counted down the fifty heartbeats they knew was the minimum time to reload a ship-borne catapult. And Rome's harpax weapons were designed for close-quarter attack, where the bolts were fired with such power that they could penetrate the enemy's superstructure to cause havoc within.

They surged onward, *Hera* in the lead.

But now, as more fireballs were flung towards them, several enemy ships had identified the danger and closed around Mark Antony's flagship. Myron cursed, realising the direct route was about to be cut off. Between them now lay a quinquereme, not the biggest of the enemy fleet but an obstacle nonetheless. He was about to order a slight change of course when Rome suffered its first casualty, a fireball smashing into one of the towers on *Minerva*'s deck not far astern of *Hera*. The tower remained standing, but if the flames caught hold the men at its crown would die horribly. Some were already leaping to the deck and as the tower leaned, others fell into the sea.

Myron did not need to watch. Agrippa's ship would survive; losing men was inevitable in any war, although fire was the cruellest death. He caught the eye of Eurycles, and a silent understanding passed between them — they must fight through the shield of ships to reach Mark Antony. No one said it would be easy. And now those ships protecting their master had seen the success of just one hit and redoubled their efforts, sending a steady stream of fireballs at the approaching ships. Now, as the range closed, their *ballistae* opened up with flaming missiles that streaked across the wave tops. As *Hera* was bow on to this threat, she presented a small target, yet still she took heavy blows close to where her forward harpax was armed and ready. The ship shuddered and ignored the wounding; bow spray would dowse all flames there.

If Myron and Eurycles had turned to watch, they would have witnessed the loss of a Roman trireme shadowing *Minerva* and the destruction of a *liburnian* similar in size to *Hera*. But both men were focused on the enemy quinquereme that now lay between them and the murderer of Eurycles' father. And their helmsmen, Niko and Shoeless, knew exactly what was in their captain's mind. They steered as close to the wind as they dared, building speed and approaching from an angle astern of the enemy. In *Hera*'s bows and stern, the harpax teams were attuned and ready. Laris's archers found every gap available to them along the port flank. Ratboy and Panther were unafraid and held fast to the rigging, willing their ship onwards. Zara, too, was shouting encouragement.

Hera swept in at speed and took out the enemy's oars, which splintered in disarray. The heavy oar handles smashed into the backs of the quinquereme's rowers, crushing ribs and skulls, immediately ending the ship's effectiveness. At the same time, *Hera*'s bow harpax fired a flaming dart into the heart of the quinquereme just below the command deck and reloaded in time to send another missile into her forward quarters. The stern harpax did the same and as *Hera* swept past, enemy soldiers, aghast at the damage the attacker was causing, fired a feeble volley of spears and arrows that touched none of the Greek crew.

Now *Hera*'s sail lost the wind as she came within range of Mark Antony's flagship, which did not hesitate to launch a broadside of her own. Fire and arrows rained on the little ship, and Myron had no choice but to signal a sharp turn away from the threat. She survived the fires but two rowers slid sideways into colleagues, pierced in their chests by arrows. Zara saw this and scrambled to help lay out the victims and staunch the flow of blood. Following their lead, *Minerva* and four other ships were closing on the knot of vessels surrounding Mark Antony, taking their lead from the plucky Greek vessel.

Myron ordered his helmsmen to heave to and his rowers to rest. Now out of range of the fire missiles, both he and Eurycles knew that the secret of success in a war at sea was to know your enemy's strengths and weaknesses. The captain took a moment to survey the battle scene. All around the centre commanded by Arruntius, ships were engaging to hurl fire and iron at each other, some seeking to ram the larger enemy vessels, others adopting harrying tactics to slow the advance.

Eurycles was controlling his emotions. 'What have we learned?' he asked Myron.

'That their catapults are inaccurate and their close-quarter weapons are bows, arrows and spears.'

'Whereas ours are fire-breathing harpax.'

Both men nodded in agreement. But Eurycles had more to say.

'A single ship attacking these giants cannot win,' he said, almost apologetically. 'Look around. Agrippa's tactics are right. Several ships attacking each enemy ship in turn like a pack of dogs on a deer — that will win the day.'

They looked down at the rowing decks, where Zara was bathing the wounded men with sea water brought by Ratboy and extracting arrowheads amid the victims' cries of pain. The rowers watched in concerned silence, passing waterskins for each to drink deeply.

'We may lose more men because we are not well protected,' said Myron. 'But we can win this fight because our weapons are better. And you are right; we must work as a team. Even if it means we are not the ones to exact revenge on Mark Antony.'

Eurycles turned to address the crew. 'Men of *Hera*, men of Laris the Brave, we have only just begun. We have just proved that we are the better seamen and the better fighters. We have destroyed an enemy ship —' he pointed to the heat of the sea-battle — 'but there are hundreds more. We are better than them, we have a greater cause, and out there are cruel men who murdered my father and who seek to put you all under the yoke of slavery. We are free men, and we are here to fight for that freedom. If it is true that more ships follow these, all laden with treasure, and we can defeat them, then not only will you be free as Rome has promised, but you will all be rich beyond your dreams. Are you with me?'

There was a moment of silence on the crew deck while around them the din of sea warfare raged. Then a lone voice, deep and resonant, simply said, 'Aye.' Everyone immediately joined the acclamation.

'Aye!' they shouted in unison.

Eurycles looked fondly upon them all.

'Then, men of Taenarum and you, followers of Laris the Etruscan, let us show these pitiful pretenders that they are not welcome here, this is our sea, and all of their wrongs will be righted tenfold.'

The men cheered.

'But now we go again into danger and fearsome onslaught. I do not know what is in the minds of the gods, but I have faced them with this brave woman.' He pointed down to where Zara tended the stricken men. 'Together we have looked Apollo in the eye, and he returned us to you. Why would he do this if we are not to fulfil his will? Men, the gods have spoken. The enemy may try to kill you, but all of you are under the protection of Apollo himself.'

The resulting cheer could probably be heard in Actium.

CHAPTER TWENTY-SEVEN

The loss of the quinquereme had been a severe blow to Mark Antony's strategy. It had been positioned to shield him from the enemy's fire darts, and now a pesky little ship with a Greek eye on its bow had scythed its oars and set it on fire.

How dare they, thought Antony as he snapped his fingers and commanded a refill for his wine goblet. He turned it in his hands, admiring the pure gold workmanship and the precious gems set into it, then looked around at the shimmering beauty of his pavilion, the billowing oriental material woven in his colours, blue and gold.

'Send the captain to me,' he growled at his servant. 'Now.'

The servant scurried off to find the ship's commanding officer, thinking of how he had come to detest his master almost as much as he loathed being at sea, captive to the stench of sweat and vomit that seeped up from the rowing decks below. Life had been almost tolerable in Mark Antony's land headquarters, but now this folly of cramming soldiers into an oversized wooden tub was too much to bear. He knew he would die in these grey seas, probably drowning alone while crying out for his beloved wife and children back home in Ephesus. He picked his way through the ranks of soldiers, pinching his nose against the stink, to the forward catapult placement where the captain was berating the engineering detail for not fixing the firing mechanism quickly enough. After several attempts to attract the officer's attention — he wouldn't dare tap him on his finely armoured shoulder, nor tug the hem of his embroidered vest — he managed to convince him that the supreme commander wanted to see him urgently.

He led the officer along the crowded deck, shouting 'make way' above the rhythmic groaning of a hundred oars, the deep boom of a timing drum and the curses of soldiers jostling for space on the disorganised upper deck. They gave a working catapult a wide berth as soldiers, stripped to the waist, winched a firing arm into position ready to be loaded with a pitch-soaked projectile and ignited by one of the nearby torchbearers. They passed ranks of archers and slingers who would rain down death on any ship that came within range.

Mark Antony's shipboard pavilion always disgusted the officer, a true navy man who had longed for action throughout the long months of posturing in the Ambracian Gulf. That new material from the orient probably cost more than the fine furniture and ornate tableware and was more suited to a palace garden. *Wine jugs and cups will soon be rolling on the deck when the wind gets up*, he thought, *if your fancy tent isn't burned to a cinder first*.

Mark Antony had his back to them, his powerful arms placed on his favourite Parthian table, as ornately carved as the goblet beside him was bejewelled. Through parted curtains, he watched the flotilla of enemy ships converging on his flagship. He did not look up or acknowledge the officer's arrival.

'Why are we not firing on those ships?'

Then he turned and stared with fiery eyes at the captain, who courageously held his gaze. The servant tried to stand still, looking down, but his quivering legs betrayed him.

'Answer me!' shouted Mark Antony.

The captain took a deep breath to control his anger. 'Sir, they are too far away. But that one —' he pointed to a trireme that was closing fast, followed by several others — 'that one is almost in range.'

'Then go and sink it. What are you waiting for?'

The officer turned to obey, but Mark Antony called him back.

'Where is the queen and her ships?'

'I can show you, Sir, if you wish.'

For a moment, the officer thought he might have overstepped the mark, implying that Antony only had to use his eyes to see that Cleopatra, Queen of Egypt, had brought her monstrous ships out through the straits. These were now anchored in the shallows just out of range of Octavian's shore artillery, all sixty of them. He felt inclined to treat the world-renowned former triumvir like a child and lead him to the stern to show him what was going on all around him. But he resisted. Instead, he bowed and indicated a good place to observe.

The two men walked to the stern, where teams of sailors manned four huge steering paddles, all linked together with ropes and pulleys. The breeze toyed with Mark Antony's dark hair, and he stumbled as his flagship rolled gently in the rising swell. The sailors saluted as one but immediately resumed their grip on the heavy tillers. The captain took him to the very edge of the steering platform and pointed east to where his queen's ships, huge and menacing and carrying the wealth of his future empire, were seemingly stationary against the land mass behind them. He nodded his approval.

Just then, three catapults loosed with the startling crack of the firing arms clattering against crossbeams, and he turned to see the machines lurch back with the kick of a mule. He tracked the trajectories of three smoking balls towards the oncoming ships to starboard, willing them to strike home. One did, crashing onto the deck of one of the ships in a burst of flames; the others missed. Mark Antony resisted the temptation to clap his hands in triumph. The officer allowed himself a smile, but he was a realist — their Roman opponents were led by a man who knew how to win a sea-battle.

Almost immediately, the oncoming ships opened fire and flaming bolts streaked towards them. Three found their mark below the deck where they stood, and they could hear the cries of pain and anguish as men died at their oars.

'Sir, I must attend to the men and assess the damage.'

Mark Antony nodded, his expression one of dismay. 'Go,' he said, and as the officer strode away he shouted after him, 'Have your catapults and *ballistae* redouble their efforts! For every dart the enemy fire, I want ten returned.'

Then he saw the smoke forcing its way between the deck's planks.

A surge of anger swept over him, stirring his blood and reminding him that he was the man who had brought triumph after triumph to Rome, in Gaul, at Pharsalus, at Philippi, and in Armenia. Parthia? Forget Parthia — that wasn't his fault. Now they were in this mess in disease-ridden Greece and forced to fight at sea just to get away to regroup. How ignominious.

He pulled himself together and swore that upstart pretender Octavian would pay for this. He looked midships, where his men crowded ready to fight, and using the height of the steering platform, he addressed them. He didn't need to get their attention by shouting or crashing sword on shield or any such thing; the soldiers massed before him had sensed his presence. He looked into the eyes of those nearest then shifted his gaze to those beyond.

'It does not matter whether we fight on land or at sea, for I am your commander,' he began. 'A child comes against a man. Rome is delusional, lost and wasted in its politics and fading memories of former glory. I am the true inheritor of Gaius Julius Caesar's legacy and the man to rescue Rome from the greed and corruption of a pathetic senate. Today we will sink her feeble ships and restore a Rome that honours its people and in particular its noble soldiers.'

He paused for cheers and applause. But there was none. Instead, everyone ducked involuntarily as a volley of flaming bolts screamed just above their heads. Mark Antony fumed. He knew he had lost the moment and now he looked to starboard, where more ships seemed to be moving towards him. The flagship's catapults loosed more missiles, but the enemy was too close now and the fireballs sailed harmlessly above the lead ships. Archers and slingers pressed to the rails to fight at last, even if only to fire on smaller ships as they came ever closer.

Mark Antony tried to resume his speech. 'Men, hear me...' he began, but he had lost them. Or rather, Octavian's fighting ships had stolen their attention. He had left it too late to use his grand oratory to spur men on to victory.

He knew what he had to do.

CHAPTER TWENTY-EIGHT

Eurycles watched as one of Agrippa's triremes used the same tactics as *Hera* had employed moments earlier. It took a wide sweep from astern the huge flagship and scythed into the twin banks of oars. But in doing so, the smaller ship was exposed to a barrage of arrows, spears and slingshots and next him, Zara hid her eyes from what must have been a devastating torrent of death and brutal injury.

Next came another of Agrippa's ships, which fired two harpax grappling irons into the same places on her flanks where flaming bolts had just been fired. Flames now licked around oar ports, and dense smoke fanned in the breeze. The grappling hooks were winched taut and men on the broken ship began to hack at the ropes, but they were protected by long iron sheaths. Yet the huge ship did not slow, despite the efforts of the attacking trireme's rowers. The smaller vessel was now being dragged alongside, yielding it open to the archers on the decks above. As arrows, slingshots and even boulders rained down on the smaller ship, men severed the harpax ropes that they had hoped would enable them to capture such a great prize. That tactic had failed.

'They should keep going with the fire bolts,' said Myron. 'Maybe ram them, too. When they are stopped or sinking, then they can be boarded and captured.'

Eurycles murmured his agreement. Both men were new to sea warfare on this scale and against such large vessels. But they were fast learners. Beyond their personal fight with Mark Antony, a dozen or more ships were ablaze, most of them the enemy's. The strengthening breeze fanned the flames pumped into the huge targets by relentless harpax broadsides. On the burning ships, men fought the fires with their supplies of drinking water and sought to hoist seawater in buckets. But their efforts were disorganised and increasingly futile as men milled in confusion, and many unfortunates screamed in agony as flames took them. Some, in desperation, threw themselves overboard without stopping to think of the impossibility of surviving in full armour and heavy boots.

The next trireme to home in on Mark Antony's ship charged in at right angles, on a clear ramming course. Smoke was now billowing from two places below her main deck, yet still she fired her great catapults, more in hope than tactical judgement. As the Roman ship closed, Eurycles reminded Myron that *Hera* would be next in line to attack. He wanted to be as close to the murderer of his father as possible when and if the time came for hand-to-hand combat.

'We are too small to ram such a large ship,' he said to Myron, 'but my bet is that she will soon hoist sails to run from this swarm of wasps. We need to stop their escape. Any ideas?'

Myron knew exactly what to do. He was certain that Eurycles did too. He looked towards the enemy ship as the smaller trireme closed in on her midships and watched the first volley of arrows seeking out the attacker's rowers in a bid to put them off their stroke. Then he looked at the stern command platform, where a fancy pavilion stood next to the huge steering shafts, four of them, manned by a dozen sailors. *That is where Mark Antony sits*, he thought and looked to Eurycles. Both men nodded in unspoken agreement.

Two things happened in rapid succession. Just a heartbeat before the trireme's beak struck home, a catapult loosed and a ball of fire looped skywards. Every man on board *Hera* craned their necks to watch its trajectory. They held their breath. The oar blades were left where they lay, dipped in the swell. Myron was first to react.

'Starboard stroke! Now!' he cried.

The men on that side needed no second command. They heaved and *Hera* turned sharply. They heaved again, and the port-side rowers held their blades steady in the water to aid their turn. The sound of the fireball was something between a fluttering and a rumble as it fell just two spear lengths from the stern. It hissed as it landed in the swirling slack water left by the ship's frantic turn to safety — right where *Hera* would have been if not for Myron's command.

The relief was palpable. That would have killed a dozen men and reduced *Hera* to a blazing wreck of confusion, probably destroying its sails and putting the brave ship out of action. Eurycles congratulated Myron with a slap to the shoulder. Zara had covered her face with her hands. But in the bows, the two boys and Laris were pointing to their target. Rome's trireme had succeeded in ramming Mark Antony's flagship, and its crew were now back-rowing to free themselves. They were at the mercy of the archers on board Antony's flagship. The screams of the dying and wounded carried back across the water. The trireme would be fortunate to survive for another attack, but what of the flagship that Agrippa had so eagerly targeted to swing the battle in his favour? Yes, it had slowed, and was it beginning to list? Those timbers were thick and strong, but perhaps they had been split or at least weakened on the waterline.

There was no time to stand and stare. Myron ordered the rowers to resume and spoke to his helmsmen, Niko and Shoeless. They understood his plan and without hesitation held *Hera* on a gradual turn. They knew exactly where to steer. As helmsmen, they knew the value of this precious part of a ship's operation.

She picked up speed towards the stern of the now ruined enemy flagship. In *Hera*'s bows, and at the stern next to the grimly determined steersmen, two harpax teams armed their weapons. Men stood by with torches aflame, ready to light bolts wrapped with oil-infused cloths. In the bows, Laris and his men nocked arrows. Everyone knew what the plan was without waiting for instruction.

The little ship cut a course that would pass perilously close to the stern of the giant ship. The closer, the more deadly. Myron saw men on the enemy vessel come alert to the danger as archers hustled towards its stern, but he knew they would be too late. On that vast command platform, he saw the unmistakable figure of Mark Antony come to the railings to see for himself the approaching danger. He was shouting to his men and waving his arms. Nearby servants were frozen in terror. The mouse had come against the lion.

The first bolt crashed into the superstructure just below his feet and he retreated. The look of terror was apparent on the faces of the flagship's steersmen. Two of them panicked and left their station at a sprint just as Laris's archers loosed their first volley. They survived, and so did Mark Antony, who threw himself to the deck, but four fell. The steering detail was down to half-strength, not an impossible crisis, but the Greek *liburnian* had more to offer. She passed close to the stern, her second *ballista* loosed and another volley of arrows flew, although the enemy stern was so high they had no clear view of those above them. They aimed more in hope than expectation, but the flaming harpax missile pierced the ship's stern, where it would set a fire in the steering mechanisms. At the same time, *Hera*'s forward harpax managed one more shot, which found its home. Even as she passed beneath the enemy stern, Myron knew that masterful teamwork had ended the life of their primary target, even if their attack would take time to have its effect.

Laris ordered a further volley as *Hera* heeled away and the last of the steersmen ran, three more dropping under the onslaught. All of the crew were looking back at what they had done — except for Zara.

'Look there!' she called. All nearby turned to look where she pointed towards the land, where the Egyptian fleet had remained at anchor throughout these exchanges. Signals were flying at their masts, sails unfurling. Sixty ships were joining the fray. Or were they?

All around *Hera* ships engaged, some burning but many still locked in furious firefights. Trumpets sounded, men cried their last, and more ships floundered low in the water. Who could tell which side had the upper hand? Mark Antony's fleet continued its remorseless onward course, despite a seriously damaged flagship in which hungry flames were fanned by the wind.

And now the Egyptians were coming.

CHAPTER TWENTY-NINE

Lucius Gellius Publicola was in a bad mood. He was in a lot of pain. Those Greek bastards had put an arrow in his knee. He could still hobble, but the throbbing pain had now reached his groin and he wondered if the arrowhead had been poisoned. He wouldn't put it past those barbaric Greeks.

But there was another pain, and this one was gnawing at his gut. That manipulative Egyptian queen in her floating palace — he couldn't bring himself to call it a ship, not by any stretch of the imagination — made his blood boil. What in Jupiter's name did Mark Antony see in her? She was all flouncing arrogance and kohl-darkened eyes. She was dripping in jewellery and had a retinue of a hundred slaves just to carry her wardrobe — and she paraded this in front of a half-starved army. Now her golden barge was wallowing in sheltered waters, surrounded by equally pretentious foreign ships, none of which had ever seen warfare at sea — he was certain of that. For the queen, it was a glorious day out. She would be enjoying the sunshine and having a picnic on deck while watching the spectacle of real men in real warships fighting to the death with fire and sword. He half expected to hear a ripple of applause float across the short distance between her ship and his whenever an enemy vessel was hit by a fireball.

He had protested as furiously as he dared when Mark Antony had ordered him to stay with the Egyptian fleet as a naval guard for Cleopatra, because her ships carried treasure beyond description. The Eastern Alliance's coffers contained enough coin to pay the troops — if ever they were so lucky — and gold, silver and jewels besides. Of course, he knew all about the plan to flee when the opportunity arose, and of course he would stay as close to all that money as he could, but he was a fighting general, and his sword itched to bite into an enemy's flesh. Especially if he got close to that Spartan peasant he had so enjoyed torturing. *Should have cut off more than a finger*, he thought to himself.

His gaze fell on the caged man. This Strabo character was important to so many of his enemies, not least the woman — his *sister*, no less. He would make her watch while he carved pieces out of him then have his pleasure with her. Or perhaps he'd make Strabo watch while his men enjoyed the woman then kill them both. One way or another, his opportunity would come because he held Strabo captive, and the Greeks and *that woman* would try to save him. In the meantime, he would use the pathetic wretch as a human shield because he also knew how important he was to Octavian and Agrippa.

He hobbled closer to the cage and studied his almost-naked captive. Strabo huddled in the corner of his suspended cage like a terrified animal, his sun-scorched skin raw and blistering, peeling lips swollen and dry. Loose excrement dribbled beneath his soiled loincloth. Publicola grinned; he enjoyed moments like this.

'Thirsty?' he asked.

Strabo was unable to speak through his parched lips. He simply held out a pleading hand.

Better keep him alive, the general thought and turned to call to an officer to bring water. But he was distracted. There was something happening on the queen's ship. New signal pennants were being hoisted, and a team of well-dressed sailors were manning the anchor winch. Others dashed busily on the decks, obeying orders barked in their garbled foreign tongue. Teams were manhandling sails into position, ready to hoist on twin masts. The ship was readying for departure, and now he saw that others in the Egyptian fleet were doing exactly the same.

But he had been kept in the dark. Was he not the most senior officer, and why had this upstart queen not asked his permission? He called for the watch officer, a young tribune who came running. Even before the tribune had saluted, Publicola was berating him.

'Explain,' said Publicola tersely, pointing to the Egyptian flagship, *Antonia*.

'Sir, we were not informed. I apologise.'

'I'll deal with you later. If you want the skin to remain on your back, call across to that ship and find out what's going on.' The tribune saluted and turned to obey, but Publicola called him back. 'And have the ship's captain prepare to set sail.'

He ignored the confusion of the crew and soldiers stirring themselves for some kind of action and looked across the bay to where the battle raged, trying to make sense of what he saw. At this distance, it was difficult to make out individual ships, but he could see that dozens of vessels were ablaze and there appeared to be several knots of ship-to-ship engagement. It was impossible to tell who had the upper hand. But was there a gap in the centre, where there was less smoke and fewer ships? Was that what Cleopatra had seen? *She should have consulted me before making sail, rather than acting on a whim as women do.*

The tribune returned, panting and sweating profusely in his dress uniform.

'Sir, the queen has decided that all is lost and wishes to sail back to her land.'

Publicola choked. 'The queen has decided…? What does she know of sea warfare?'

The tribune noticed that his commanding officer was clenching and unclenching his fists and wished he had the courage to speak out: *Actually, Sir, none of us have that knowledge.* But he didn't dare. He took a step back and waited for orders. None came. There was just the madness of a ship readying for action.

Given its lavish appearance, the queen's ship may have been more suited to state ceremonials, but Publicola found himself impressed with the slick performance of the royal crew. Five hundred oarsmen brought *Antonia* about, and her sails caught the promising breeze. She was already picking up speed even before Publicola's ship had weighed and stowed anchor. This would not do. He screamed at the tribune to do better, whip the men, threaten them with fearful punishment.

The tribune bit back a rueful smile as he pretended to obey and saw the resentment and brewing discontent in the eyes of those nearest. *He doesn't even know my name*, he thought to himself as he ordered the mainsail hoisted. It had been bad enough serving under Publicola with his unpredictability and penchant for cruel punishments, but now with a wounded knee the general had become even more dangerous, if that was possible. *Shame that arrow hadn't been a cubit higher for an even more agonising gut wound and a slow death*, the tribune thought. He would gladly have twisted the shaft to heighten the pain, and he knew most of the men would have done the same. Probably his fellow officers too. And now here they all were, trapped on this stinking ship with meagre rations and little water, ordered to sail into the horror of a naval battle — and for what? Control of Rome? Pah! He should have got out long ago with those other defectors.

The ship had managed to find its course, even without his full attention. Perhaps the general had some experience of commanding a warship after all. He now had her pointing towards the sea battle, albeit some distance behind the leading Egyptians. Publicola was berating the officers on his command deck, who in turn were calling for more speed to catch up with Cleopatra's *Antonia*. The tribune busied himself with the mainsail's trim; the great sail's sheets had become tangled, and it flapped uselessly as he helped the sailors push their way among disgruntled marines to unravel the offending ropes. Any moment now Publicola's wrath would be unleashed on him. Below, the drums beat a rhythm for three hundred oarsmen, and this seemed sufficient diversion for commanders until a gust caught the sail, pulling the port sheets taut and sweeping a fully armoured soldier overboard.

Publicola glared down at the main deck, looking for someone to blame. The tribune busied himself making the ropes fast while keeping his back to the angry general. He could feel the intensity of those grey eyes like a spear between his shoulders. What did he expect with so many men crammed onto this floating death-trap? But the mainsail now filled, and the general's anger never came. The tribune risked a glance back at the command deck, where the officers were all preoccupied with avoiding other ships in the convoy, so he made his way forward to check the anchor had been stowed properly. Anything to put distance between himself and the general.

He sat on a rope coil and looked up at the poor wretch in the cage suspended above the bows. The man was near death. Talk among shipmates was that the prisoner was a spy who had been caught recording troop numbers, but the fact that he hadn't been summarily executed indicated he must be important in some way, perhaps useful if the time came for bargaining or a prisoner exchange. The man reached a hand through a space between the canes. The tribune stood, unstopped his waterskin and passed it up to him. He smiled as the prisoner drank greedily.

'Steady, go easy,' said the tribune.

The man passed the skin back. He was filthy and blistered. His mouth contorted in an effort to speak, but he managed only a croak of gratitude.

The tribune sat again and took a welcome drink himself. 'I don't know who you are,' he said, 'but let's face it, we're both prisoners on this wretched ship.'

CHAPTER THIRTY

Standing together, Eurycles and Myron studied the oncoming Egyptian fleet. *Hera* was among those closest to the new threat after making her successful pass across Mark Antony's stern, and now she had turned her bows into the wind, sail lowered, to assess the next move.

The sight was frightening. There were sixty enormous ships, none of them by any stretch of the imagination fast — they were solid, broad and cumbersome — but with a following wind that had strengthened throughout the afternoon, their progress was relentless. Ramming them would be no more than a mosquito bite. Attempting to shatter their thick oars, each manned by up to ten slaves, would probably cause more damage to the attacker than the Egyptians. Fire bolts? Ineffectual against the thick hides of such monsters. And *Hera* was right in their path.

'We know what they are going to do,' said Eurycles, 'or at least we think we know.'

Myron raised an eyebrow. 'Seems obvious to me,' he said. 'Rome's ships will be lucky to take even one or two of them out as they sail right through the lines to open sea.'

'And when they do, they have their sails and Rome's ships do not, so a chase would be futile.' Eurycles looked across the deck to where the purple sail had been furled. 'Perhaps Agrippa will have a task for us if they break through, as we're the only ship under sail?'

Myron sighed. 'To follow? That's about all we could do.'

Both turned to see what was happening around them. A pall of thick smoke drifted south across increasingly choppy seas.

Ships burned and others wallowed as the seas claimed them. Fireballs and pots of flaming pitch arced randomly, and fierce fighting had erupted where ships had locked together with grappling irons. The roar of hundreds of men thrown into frantic combat mingled with the screams of the dying. The great struggle for land supremacy was taking place on the ocean. It was chaotic and murderous.

'Or we can sail straight back to Taenarum,' said a wistful Eurycles.

'Not while I'm here,' said a female voice behind them. They hadn't noticed Zara's approach. Her eyes flashed with determination. 'Over there —' she pointed to the raging battle — 'is the man who murdered your father.' Now she pointed to the approaching Egyptian fleet. 'And over there, if you look carefully, is the ship under the command of the man who holds my brother captive. The same man who mutilated you, Eurycles, and who did unspeakable things to us both.'

Both men looked where she pointed. And there, under sail and oar, was a smaller ship that bore no resemblance to the Egyptian vessels. It was nestled among the larger ships but was clearly capable of more speed than those around. Like all of those in the approaching fleet, it had divested itself of the artillery tower, tossing it into the sea to allow more nimble seamanship and pace in flight, confirming that was the plan. Clear on its foredeck was the ugly cage that held Strabo captive.

Eurycles felt guilty. He was tired, so tired, and he didn't know what to say to Zara. He missed his home, and the fury of vengeance had all but passed. But now he drew on Zara's gritty determination to save her brother, whether or not that meant exacting revenge on evil men. He wanted to match her resolve.

It was the least he could do after all they had been through. He opened his mouth to reply, but Zara had more to say.

'If you will not at least try, I will leap overboard and swim there to do it myself.'

Shoeless had heard the exchange and gave a hollow laugh, then silenced himself when she locked her gaze on him. She then turned to the crew at the oars, to the archers crouched ready in the bows, and proved herself an orator as well as a courageous warrior.

'What do you men think?' she asked, her voice rising above the distant clamour of war. 'We have all suffered at the hands of these madmen who come here with their legions and their great ships. This is not my land, it is yours, but I stand with you to oppose this horror, this rape and murder of the innocents, this shameful war that has no bearing on you and me except that powerful men think nothing of our lives in their lust for glory and land. What will you do? Will you meekly turn the other cheek and be struck again and again by the fist of corruption, or will you stand with me and fight them — to the death, if needs be?'

The men murmured their approval, but while she had been speaking two youths had made their way among the rowers and now approached the command deck. Ratboy and Panther, Zara's devoted teenagers, stood before her. Ratboy was skinny and untidy in his ill-fitting and fraying clothes, while Panther managed to look athletic and muscular beyond his years. Both bowed and placed their long knives on the deck before her.

'Lady, if you swim to save your brother, we will swim with you,' said Panther.

'We will,' echoed Ratboy.

Zara embraced them both. The crew cheered. But they were silenced by a command from Myron.

'Come about, hoist sail.'

Right now, they were in the way of the oncoming leviathans, like ants in the path of an elephant herd. Not a good place to be. But *Hera* was nimble and quick, capable of dancing between these great ships and dodging their missiles. Yes, they would seek out Publicola if they could, but first they must find Agrippa's flagship *Minerva* to report their intentions.

Eurycles studied the raging battle stretched across two miles of open sea. He was looking for Agrippa's ship but smoke and wreckage made it impossible to pick out individual ships. From this distance, there appeared to be three main engagements, left, right and centre, with no obvious indication of who was winning. It was a bitter and furious sea battle in which thousands would be losing their lives even as they watched. Then Myron pointed to a larger vessel, listing and streaming black smoke from her stern decks. Several small messenger pinnaces buzzed around her, nipping between the attacking *liburnians* and triremes to add to the confusion. Perhaps to evacuate survivors? Even Mark Antony himself?

'If that's Antony's flagship going down, that's where Agrippa will be,' he said.

'Go there,' said Eurycles, 'but sinking his ship is not enough. I want the man who killed my father.'

Under oars and with the mainsail as close-hauled as they dared, *Hera* made for the melee to look for Mark Antony. Behind them, sixty Egyptian ships under full sail with a following wind were now breaking for the two gaps in the strung-out battle, revealing their intentions. They were making a run for it, and there was little the Roman fleet would be able to do about it. Agrippa might have judged this to be a feint; the Egyptians could pass through the lines and then double back to attack the Romans from behind. It could be a classic pincer movement, just like cavalry tactics in a land battle. But Myron knew this was unlikely. Monstrous ships like Cleopatra's were not given to manoeuvrability. They were running, and he knew it.

They came closer to the listing ship and knew it was Mark Antony's. Black smoke was cascading from the stern decks, her steering gear abandoned and blackening in the flames. Rome's ships were making passes with more bolts and a hailstorm of arrows, and the enemy was in distressed confusion as soldiers sought escape on the small boats that came close enough. Others took their chances by jumping into the churning waters where they would drown, weighed down by armour and heavy land-boots. Several dark fins circled, the great fish drawn by the scent of human blood. Zara shuddered at the scene while the crew watched, aghast.

All except Myron and Eurycles, and with them Ratboy, who searched the faces and dress uniforms for the man they sought. So they did not see the Egyptian fleet nose confidently through the lines as they set course to the south-east, driven by a strengthening wind that swirled offshore from the Pindus mountains of Epirus. Nor did they see Agrippa's ship *Minerva* emerge from a bank of thick smoke until she swept around the wreckage, almost within oar-touching distance of *Hera*.

'Men of Taenarum!' It was Agrippa himself who hailed them through cupped hands. 'Men of Taenarum, you are all true heroes…' His next words were lost in the surrounding shouts and cries of anguish coming from the stricken flagship.

'Mark Antony?' Eurycles called back.

'Not seen,' came the reply. 'No doubt he's escaped in disguise. But I have one more task for you and your brave men.'

'We are yours to command,' returned Eurycles. *But only until the gods grant us opportunity for our true purpose here*, he thought.

Agrippa pointed to where the last of the Egyptian ships could be seen in the distance, their sails filled, their purpose clear.

'Only your ship!' yelled Agrippa as this vessel slid past. 'You are the only one with sails. Follow them and observe. You will all be paid handsomely.'

CHAPTER THIRTY-ONE

Finding a route through the mayhem demanded seamanship of the highest order. But Myron was up to the task, especially with Niko and Shoeless at the steering oars. This was so different to navigating a busy harbour or chasing shoals of tunny. It required watchful eyes fore and aft as blazing pitch flew through the air all around, and discerning friend from foe was not easy in the chaos.

Ratboy and Panther had been sent to the bows with instructions to watch their course ahead and use hand signals to alert Myron to dangers near and far. Wrecked ships floundered and men lay in the water, clinging to lost spars and flotsam, and knots of enemy warships lay ahead. *Hera*'s crew ignored plaintive cries from the murky waters below her bows; a greater purpose was now at hand. But none knew where it would lead them.

Laris and his men were ordered to rest. Their skills would be needed later, a handful of skilled bowmen and two harpax *ballistae* their only weapons against sixty enormous Egyptian ships. Not great odds. But no one dissented.

Zara brought water to Eurycles and the helmsmen. She leaned on him wearily.

'Where now?'

None of them knew the answer.

As they eventually broke free from the wreckage of war to set a course to follow the Egyptians, Laris came to the command deck to report.

'It's not good,' he told Eurycles and Myron. 'We have few arrows left to us and only four bolts for the scorpios. And no pitch or oil for the fires.'

Eurycles sighed. 'All we can do is try,' he said wearily.

Zara was indignant, not for the first time. 'Your god Apollo has brought us thus far. Ask yourself why that is. Is he not as powerful as the sun itself, burning bright with endeavour and vengeance? Must I berate you again for your lack of faith?'

Myron studied his feet. Eurycles watched sixty ships on their southerly course past the island of Leukas and drew Zara close. 'As I said, we try,' he whispered in her ear.

Niko and Shoeless concentrated on a pursuing course.

Hera was fast and soon shortened sail as she closed on the fleeing Egyptians. The rowers were ordered to ship oars and rest. After the horror and intensity of all they had witnessed, a silence descended on *Hera*'s crew. Rations and waterskins were shared. The intrusion of gulls mistaking them for fishermen brought a welcome change to the battle-fury that had assaulted them for several hours. A school of dolphins played their games in the ship's bow-waves.

Zara shrugged off Eurycles' arm and made for the bows, where Ratboy and Panther watched the way ahead. She murmured thanks and encouragement to the rowers as she passed them, appreciative of their efforts and asking for one more effort when the time came. She found the teenagers and saw the firm set of their jaws, the determination in their eyes. They shared her lust for vengeance, and she was glad of it.

'Can you see him?' she asked them.

They knew what she meant.

'Think so,' said Panther, who had spent much of his young life watching suspicious nobles and corrupt officers. 'Right in the middle of that fleet. Hiding, probably.'

'Hiding from us?'

Ratboy snorted. 'Nowhere to hide. We're coming for him.'

'One ship? Against sixty?'

'We'll find a way,' said Ratboy, and Panther agreed.

'Look,' said Zara, 'if we catch up with that bastard, you two must stay safe. Keep out of trouble. Leave it to the men. I need both of you to come through this.'

Both youngsters were fuelled by the hope and expectation of youth. 'We will, lady, we will,' said Panther. 'But if we can rescue Strabo and bring you Publicola's head, all the better.'

Zara shook her head. 'We're here to follow and watch, nothing more.'

Panther didn't take his eyes off their quarry.

'If you follow someone closely enough, eventually they'll turn. And when he does, that's when we'll get our chance.'

Zara kissed the top of his head, and Panther blushed.

The wind that had given the fleeing Egyptians its blessing eased as the sun dropped towards the eastern horizon, throwing a soft red glow on the cliffs of Leukas island on their port side. Astern, a harsher red reflected off the clouds of smoke now stilled above the continuing struggle between East and West. The battle raged on, the cacophony of death now lost to those who sailed south.

A false sense of peace settled on *Hera* as she gradually lost headway, the only sound the gentle lapping at the waterline. Her sail was slack. The dolphins had gone to play elsewhere. But the calm was short-lived as across the short stretch of ocean came the sounds of shouted orders, the thunder of oars extended and the unhurried boom of drums to give the Egyptian rowers their timing.

Myron ordered the same pace for *Hera's* crew. He was troubled. In everything that had happened so far, he had felt confident in his ship's roaming role and that the outcome was ordained by the gods. But now he was not so sure. Their orders were to follow and observe, but for how long? They had one, maybe two hours of fading light. What then? Would the Egyptians sail on into the night, or would they put into shore? Ships rarely sailed at night — that way lay disaster, especially this close to Greece's rocky coastline. If they took the risk, they would have to carry lights so the ships could stay together, and *Hera* could follow those lights. But his crew was exhausted after, what, two days and a night of action. By all the gods, he was weary enough, so how must Eurycles and Zara feel after their ordeal? Even the energy of youth must be draining from Ratboy and Panther. Some of Laris's men dozed with bows resting on their knees; others seemed too tired to sleep, if that were possible.

Ratboy's shrill whistle made him jump. Myron had been lost in thought and now looked up. Ratboy was pointing towards the retreating Egyptians. Eurycles came to Myron's side and peered forward, where late sun flashed on the water between them and the enemy. The ghostlike vessels had not changed course and if anything had put more distance between them and their pursuer.

And then they saw what Ratboy had seen. One ship, smaller than the hulking foreigners, had detached itself from the fleet and its bows now pointed towards them, its oars rising and falling. It placed itself in their way like a single warrior holding a pass against an enemy. That, or one ship had changed its mind and given up on its Egyptian company.

Unlikely, thought Myron. This was a challenge.

He ordered oars down to slow *Hera* as they studied the ship. Its course was directly towards them, unhurried yet purposeful. Low cloud in the west parted to allow shafts of orange sunlight to illuminate the approaching vessel. It was half a mile off but now they could make out its shape, and it was familiar to them all. Not least the cage that swung lazily over its bows. A cage that held captive the brother of Zara and a friend of Rome, if Strabo was still alive.

Publicola had come to fight, and the odds were stacked heavily in his favour.

CHAPTER THIRTY-TWO

'They'll try to ram us.'

Myron spoke calmly. Eurycles was scratching at too many days of stubble. Zara hung back, leaving the seamen to decide what to do. Publicola's ship was still some way off and not yet moving at attack speed.

'We can easily dodge them,' Myron went on, 'but then what?'

Still scratching, Eurycles said, 'We have to be careful if our archers loose. We don't want to harm Strabo.'

'Loose with what? We are low on arrows. We mustn't waste them.'

'Scorpios, then? They're also in short supply, and what would we achieve?'

Eurycles found himself on the verge of admitting defeat even before the fight had begun. A tug on his jerkin stopped him giving voice to a suggestion that they keep out of range at least until darkness fell. It was Ratboy, staring up at him with crooked teeth and wild hair. He looked even more like a crazed animal than usual.

'I … we … we have a plan.'

Ever since the lad and Panther had shown such courage when rescuing him and Zara, Eurycles had looked on him with growing respect. He had always loved Ratboy and had grown fond of his friend, Panther, too. He had been made aware that both of them were mature beyond their years. Both had earned the right to be heard.

'A plan?'

Ratboy nodded. Panther stood behind him.

'Go on,' said Eurycles.

'If you can get the ship bow-to-bow and close enough, we can board that ship and rescue Strabo.'

It took a moment for Eurycles to comprehend what Ratboy was suggesting. Then he shook his head slowly. 'How will you face a century of seasoned soldiers on the deck of that ship while freeing Strabo?'

Put like that, the plan sounded impossible, but Ratboy didn't show a hint of doubt. 'With these.' Both youths tapped the long knives at their belts. They certainly looked sharp and dangerous. 'But we won't have to fight, because Laris and his men will force the soldiers to dive for cover with their arrows. We will be with Strabo in the bow, and the soldiers will cower on the deck. We will cut Strabo free. Easy.'

Eurycles thought of pointing out that Laris did not have enough arrows for more than two shots per archer, but he held his tongue. Did he have a better plan? Did Myron? No, that was clear. He turned to Myron. Both men looked up to see the enemy ship approaching, now building enough speed for white water to surge at its bows, tinted gold in the weak sunlight.

'Right, it's all we've got,' announced Eurycles.

'Wait,' said Zara, who had been listening to the exchange. 'Two boys against an army of marines?'

But Eurycles and Myron ignored her. They knew it was all they had to offer, and they had come so far through incredible difficulties. It was just one more push. And the gods were with them, especially Apollo.

'Go,' he said to the youths. 'And make sure you come back with Strabo.'

Hera presented a tempting broadside ramming opportunity to the enemy. Myron knew the theory of how this could work but it all hinged on how the whole team would work together.

Oarsmen would have to obey every command, working blind and trusting the captain. Laris's archers would need to know when to loose their few remaining arrows to pin the enemy down. And the helmsmen, Niko and Shoeless, would need to steer perfectly to avoid sacrificing their ship in a collision.

The enemy warship came on, ploughing deeper with every pull, and more ferociously now. She loomed larger and larger to all who were not engaged at an oar. Eurycles and Myron seemed outwardly calm and held the attention of every rower. Ratboy and Panther crouched like charged *ballistae* in the starboard bow. Beside them, arrayed in a double line below the starboard gunwale, were the archers, each with an arrow nocked ready and most of them with just one more each beside them. After that, they would be powerless, bar the hurling of insults.

The rowers were ready. They knew what to do. The approaching quadrireme was just two spears' length away when Myron's command came: 'Port-side back-row, starboard full ahead!'

Hera seemed to turn impossibly sharply until her bows came around to take away the enemy's hoped-for target. Their bows kissed, sending a shudder through the smaller ship. Those on the stern command deck staggered and steadied themselves against the railings, and when they looked up they saw Ratboy and Panther clinging like manic spiders to the enemy ship's bow. Above them hovered the cage containing the bedraggled figure of Strabo, who had now found sufficient reserves to stand, fists clinging to the canes of his captivity, no doubt daring to hope that his ordeal would soon end.

Hera held steady as her bows, now vacated by the two youths, struck the enemy's starboard oars one by one. But the opposite motion of the two ships was checked and although a few oars splintered, the enemy slowed almost to a halt. The two ships lay side-by-side, locked like lovers. For a moment, neither side knew what to do next.

As one, *Hera*'s archers stood and aimed right at the soldiers massed on the decks, ready to release their deadly hailstorm. They had expected exactly the same in return. But neither side loosed.

Ratboy and Panther had clambered onto the foredeck, scrambling for finger-holds and finding energy from somewhere, and were already hacking at the rope bindings that bound Strabo's cage.

On the enemy ship's stern, one officer was screaming at his archers to loose and kill the Greek vermin. On the main deck, a young officer held his arms wide, somehow holding back the deadly volley that would annihilate many of *Hera*'s bravest. Grim archers lined its deck, but their fire was withheld, as if they knew they would not fight this day.

On *Hera*, Laris saw the hesitation and screamed, 'Hold!' It was as if he had seen this kind of tension before.

Publicola screamed louder. He cursed his men. The opportunity to destroy these Greeks was passing by. He drew his sword and hurdled down to the main deck, ignoring the pain in his injured knee, and yelled curses at his men. His fellow officers on the command deck just smiled knowingly. Confused and deranged at the lack of obedience for the first time in his illustrious career with Mark Antony, he hit one archer with the flat of his sword. The archer refused to obey. Publicola stabbed him in the heart.

In the bows, Panther and Ratboy had severed several of the seawater-soaked ropes that bound the cage's canes and Strabo, summoning the effort from his drained sinews, threw all his weight downwards on the floor until it collapsed, allowing enough space to wriggle free.

Now the crews and marines on both ships were left watching each other in a bizarre stand-off. Bowstrings were taut; fingers shook and quivered on the shafts. The young officer who had started all this stared at Publicola; all the frustration of months of starvation and neglect brewed to white hot anger. He dared not say anything. He knew the penalty for what he was doing. But if he wavered now, anything might happen, and it wouldn't go well for him. He ordered his men to stand down, then turned towards Eurycles and Myron on *Hera*'s deck, and saluted.

But Publicola wasn't done.

He hobbled towards the bows, grasping a bow from an unsuspecting archer. He held out a hand for an arrow to load, calmly nocked it, aimed, and loosed.

The arrow took Panther in the chest, just as he was helping Strabo to the ship's side. A look of shock and dismay registered. He looked down at where the arrow still quivered from the impact. His legs gave way and he slid to the deck. Ratboy went to his side, cradling his friend with a great cry of despair.

Hera's archers lifted their bows as one and took aim at the massed ranks opposite. But the enemy archers did not respond. The insurgent officer commanded the ranks to stand aside, leaving Publicola standing alone on the main deck surrounded by his own, now hostile, men. But he was not finished. He screamed at them, promising decimation, castration, amputation and all the horrors a man of his standing could inflict for mutiny and rebellion. At one stage he turned back to his fellow officers on the command deck and found no support there. He looked around at his worst nightmare, the veins standing out on his neck as he yelled more bile.

The arrow took him in the neck. A clean shot. The heart of Old Rome continued to pump and crimson blood spurted across the deck, splattering the nearest rebels and the officer who commanded them. Publicola lurched backwards but remained on his feet, though not for long. His knees buckled as he dropped the bow and clutched at his neck. But not even Mark Antony's senior general could stem the flow, and now his arms and his cuirass were drenched in blood. He staggered to the side of his ship, the marines parting to allow him passage. With one final look towards Eurycles, he pitched forward and fell into the gap between the two ships.

A dark fin approached as the water was turned red by the blood of Lucius Gellius Publicola. There was a wild thrashing for several moments, and then the two ships moved together again as if a door had closed.

Zara handed the borrowed bow to Eurycles.

'Please return this to Laris with my thanks,' she said.

EPILOGUE

Dusk. Two ships leaned together where they had been beached in the shallows of a deserted cove on the island of Leukas. The Egyptian fleet had long since disappeared into the gathering night. Meddlesome seabirds had quietened, gone to their craggy roosts to rest. In the distance, towards Actium, warring ships had called off their vicious struggle for supremacy. The flames had been quenched by indignant seas, leaving the lingering smell of smoke and charred flesh hanging in the still air, even this far from the place where men had butchered, mutilated and burned each other for hour after hour.

The men of *Hera* were scavenging for wreckage and splintered oars to make a funeral pyre. Laris took three men into a wooded valley to hunt for wild boar. The young tribune and his fellow officers spoke quietly with Eurycles and Myron. The mood was subdued.

Zara wept. Her tears dampened Strabo's neck, mingling with the grime engrained in red-raw skin. They were tears of relief and sorrow. Strabo could barely speak, so neither did.

Ratboy stood alone in the shallows, brooding and allowing gentle waves to wash around him. They were cleansing the pain, if that were possible, but the water was insufficient to wash away the regret that he had not killed either of Eurycles' enemies. Shoeless found him there, ruffled his hair, and led him aside, where they sat in silence. Eventually Ratboy leaned his head on Shoeless's shoulder; they were the altar boy and the priest, the apprentice and the sailor, the child-no-more and the wild adventurer.

On the far side of the curve of yellow sand and shingle, Publicola's troops also brooded. They had been the first to create a fire to ward off the coming chill, and now they sat or crouched near the warmth, mumbling their hopes and fears for what would come next. To a man, they had hated their general for his cruelty. There had been executions and punishments — always when least expected. Seeing the look of despair in his otherwise cold eyes when they had refused to fight had been pure joy, until one of their own had been savagely despatched before their eyes. The woman whose aim had been meticulous was their new heroine. But where would they go now? Would Rome welcome them, men who had been ready to fight against the new Caesar? They had heard that he was the son of a god, and he was not known for leniency. It would all depend on who had won the battle in the seas off Actium. One thing was for sure: they were not going to Egypt. They would throw themselves on the mercy of this Caesar and trust the Greeks to put in a good word for them. Yes, they were agreed on that. And now their officers were discussing their fate with those scruffy Greek seamen. Maybe they weren't so bad. The troops had admired the two lads who had heroically leaped from ship to ship like monkeys. Perhaps they should invite such strange and plucky characters to share their fire?

The decision was taken from them when their tribune, Felix, sauntered across, the other officers and the Greeks not far behind. They liked this Felix. He had risked his life for them.

'Ah, men ... er ... we...'

'Spit it out, Sir,' said a gnarled veteran without looking up.

'Well, men, it seems we have some new friends.'

'Do we now?' said the veteran. 'So the fight's over for us?'

'It is, and what's more, these, ah, Greeks, are personal friends of Marcus Agrippa.'

'Are they now? So they will vouch for us? Or will we be led in chains through the streets of Rome just because we were in Mark Antony's pay?'

The tribune held up his hands as if to personally prevent any further misfortune befalling his troops. 'Trust me, it's true. They have given their word. But…'

'But? There's always a but,' said the veteran. 'They want something in return? There are more of us than them, and our swords are sharp…'

As he scuffed sand beneath his sandal, Felix was weighing up what his men most wanted. Riches or freedom? What if they could have both?

'Well, men,' he said, 'you know as well as I do that our ship carries two large chests in Publicola's personal cabin. You may think they contain his change of clothes and spare underwear for a long voyage to Egypt. But you would be wrong.'

The veteran wasn't stupid, and neither were the men in the tribune's hearing. Several of them stood, a new gleam in their eyes reflecting the flames in their campfire. 'Do you mean what I think you mean?'

'I do,' said the tribune. 'But we're going to share it in return for a good word from our new friends.'

Few soldiers were normally eager to share their booty, but these men mumbled to each other about their change of fortune. All along, they had sensed that they were not enjoying the favour of the gods, at least until now. Besides, someone pointed out, they had no idea just how much treasure lay stashed in their former general's closet.

'Is there wine hidden in that cabin, too?' asked the veteran.

'There might be,' came the reply. 'A couple of amphorae or three, neatly stacked in the corner.'

'Then, Sir, with apologies, what are you waiting for?'

Panther's funeral pyre blazed brightly beneath a star-studded night sky. The veteran soldier insisted on pouring a libation to a true hero, nobler than any Roman he had ever known. 'A woman with an aim as true as Diana, or Artemis if you Greeks prefer.' This was spoken with emotion only partly down to the amount of wine he had consumed.

Zara managed a smile through her tears, unseen in the darkness. Ratboy stood nearby, grim-faced, quietly thinking of how he had lost a true friend. He recalled their first meeting in Samos, so far away. It had begun with fists and aggression, yet the best friendships among the downtrodden and abused often begin that way. Shoeless stood with him, head bowed. Eurycles said a few words; no one could remember them afterwards. Then Panther was gone in the spitting fury of damp wood and the last of the pitch from Publicola's ship.

They feasted on the boars that Laris had hunted, both camps now mingling together like old friends. Disagreements were half-hearted and came to nothing. Both crews were exhausted but did their best to finish Publicola's wine, and the songs dwindled into mere mumblings.

Ratboy found Eurycles and Zara leaning wearily against the ancient trunk of a tamarisk. Dappled moonlight played on their faces, giving them a mysterious serenity, king and queen of the night. They beckoned him, and Ratboy crouched before them like a loyal servant.

'You should sleep.' Zara's voice was throaty and rich. Ratboy thought they had probably been kissing.

'Can't,' he said.

'Neither can we,' said Eurycles. 'Too much to think about.' The darkness hid his wry smile; he wasn't thinking about war and politics.

Ratboy took a deep breath. It had been on his mind ever since they had rowed ashore. 'Where is Mark Antony?'

Eurycles took his time to reply. His mission to exact revenge on the man who had murdered his father had failed. Or had it? At every turn he had helped Rome and the new Caesar to oppose Mark Antony and now, after talking to Felix at length, he knew his true enemy was defeated. Mark Antony had boarded Cleopatra's ship and fled in shame, leaving his fleet and his legions to fight without him. Dismay, defections and surrender would surely follow with the dawn when his officers learned of this.

Ratboy asked again, 'Where is he?'

'Gone.' Eurycles waved a hand in the direction of the open seas.

'We must give chase then.' In other circumstances, Ratboy's answer would have been impertinent.

Zara reached out and took Ratboy's hands in hers. She had been aware of his troubled soul ever since she had met him. He had witnessed a cruel murder in a foreign land, and such things never went away, no matter how brave the boy might pretend to be. And now he had to process the sudden death of a friend. She saw that he was biting his lip hard enough to draw blood. She wished she could draw out the pain and angst but knew that true healing would take a lifetime.

'Sometimes,' she said softly, 'you have to let go. You have done so much, my brave hero and, you know, I think there is a moment when a boy becomes a man. You came here as barely more than a child and you will leave here with us, Myron, Niko and Shoeless, as a man. I want you to show me Taenarum, your home. I would very much like to live there with my new family, away from war and pestilence. Will you take me there?'

Ratboy's emotions fought each other — the horror, the pain, the fear. The joy and laughter. The banter of *Hera*'s crew. Storm and calm. He began to shake and fought that too. He didn't want to fall apart in front of his new mother.

He fell into her arms and between sobs, managed, 'I will take you there.'

They clung to each other for a long time, with Eurycles fidgeting nearby. Eventually Zara eased herself free of the embrace.

'And another thing,' she whispered with a smile that Ratboy could barely see through tears and darkness, 'we're going to have to give you a new name.'

A NOTE TO THE READER

I was sitting outside Jack's Brasserie in Alderney's main street when I spotted a man sitting alone, reading a book. He was holding it up, elbows resting next to his latte. At that distance, I could read only one word, writ large on the hardback's cover: *ACTIUM*.

Bold as brass, I sauntered over to the man's table. 'I see you're reading about the Battle of Actium,' I said.

'I've nearly finished the book,' he replied. 'The moment I do, it's yours. But it won't give you all the answers.'

'What do you mean?'

'The thing that really puzzles me is why did Cleopatra run away after all that effort? And Mark Antony with her? And why choose to fight at sea when they outnumbered Octavian on land?'

A true historian would delve into the facts, read source material, consult peers and so on. So do good novelists, but the difference is that fiction allows a little manipulation of the facts. The book was duly borrowed: *The Battle of Actium 31BC* by Lee Fratantuono. Fratantuono forced me to return to Plutarch, Appian and Dio Cassius to find the story that would eventually lead me to write *Sea of Flames*.

It was in Plutarch that I found Eurycles: a man so enraged over the murder of his father, Lachares, that he decked out his ship at his own expense and went to war against Mark Antony. Plutarch has Eurycles pursuing Antony after the general had fled on Cleopatra's ship, announcing at the climax: 'I am Eurycles the son of Lachares, whom the fortune of Caesar enables to avenge the death of his father.' But he didn't manage to kill Antony. However, Plutarch reports success against a certain other general's ship, and there's no mention of Publicola after Actium.

There's the story, I thought.

Now, you may know more about this period of history than I do, and for my gentle manipulations, perhaps even errors, I crave your indulgence. Please, for the sake of storyline, be forgiving.

I have spent many hours researching this story, but I confess that I have shone a light brightest on the parts that help my tale of Eurycles, his plucky ship's crew, the 'cabin boy' Ratboy, Strabo the geographer, and a courageous Eastern woman named Zaramandukht.

Some of the interesting things I discovered during my research included the customary method of sacrifice at Actium: flinging victims off a cliff with birds attached to help them fly. It helped inform what Publicola might have done to Eurycles to win over the locals. And what about the strange story of Mark Antony's fleet being hindered when small sucker fish attached themselves to the keels of his ships? I've translated that as weed, worm infestation and unusual tidal flow.

Another subtle manipulation is Plutarch's and Dio's reports that Mark Antony burned around eighty of his (or Egypt's) surplus ships before the battle. The scholar W.W. Tarn argued that this was actually Octavian's doing. I've given the task to Agrippa and his fireships, which makes the story just a little more interesting, I reckon. Add to this Agrippa's harpax invention and the revolutionary use of smaller ships, and Actium suddenly becomes a tactical turning point in Roman naval history.

Finally, in addition to acknowledging the helpful café discussion that sparked this novel, I would like to thank my family, friends and fellow authors for their support and encouragement. And a special salute to Sapere Books and my editor, Natalie Linh Bolderston, for her expertise and many hours of work on *Sea of Flames*.

Reviews by knowledgeable readers are an essential part of a modern author's success, so if you enjoyed this novel I would be grateful if you could spare the short time required to post a review on **Amazon** and **Goodreads**. You can also connect with me on **Twitter** or on **my website** and **sign up to my newsletter on Substack**.

Alistair Forrest

alistairforrest.com

Sapere Books is an exciting new publisher of brilliant fiction and popular history.

To find out more about our latest releases and our monthly bargain books visit our website:
saperebooks.com

www.ingramcontent.com/pod-product-compliance
Lightning Source LLC
Chambersburg PA
CBHW060914250626
47159CB00008B/3005